"You mean you really want us to marry?"

Karen shut her eyes and wondered whether she was delirious.

"I can't think of anything that I want out of life more than that," Iain replied soberly.

Her eyes searched his face wistfully. "Are you sure it isn't pity? Pity can be very strong sometimes. And I've more or less forced you into this position. You think I'm helpless, that I need looking after. I've aroused your protective instincts—"

"Stop talking nonsense!" he said, gripping her by the shoulders, and she thought he was going to shake her.

He jerked her up almost violently into his arms, holding her helplessly crushed against him. He kissed her hair and her eyes, her soft throat and whispered, "I love you! There's no pity about it! I love you...."

OTHER
Harlequin Romances
by SUSAN BARRIE

580—NURSE NOLAN
587—HEART SPECIALIST
687—FOUR ROADS TO WINDRUSH
730—THE STARS OF SAN CECILIO
765—A CASE OF HEART TROUBLE
779—MISTRESS OF BROWN FURROWS
792—GATES OF DAWN
831—HOTEL AT TRELOAN
904—MOON AT THE FULL
926—MOUNTAIN MAGIC
967—THE WINGS OF THE MORNING
997—CASTLE THUNDERBIRD
1020—NO JUST CAUSE
1043—MARRY A STRANGER
1078—ROYAL PURPLE
1099—CARPET OF DREAMS
1128—THE QUIET HEART
1168—ROSE IN THE BUD
1189—ACCIDENTAL BRIDE
1221—MASTER OF MELINCOURT
1259—WILD SONATA
1311—THE MARRIAGE WHEEL
1359—RETURN TO TREMARTH
1428—NIGHT OF THE SINGING BIRDS
1526—BRIDE IN WAITING
2240—VICTORIA AND THE NIGHTINGALE

The House of the Laird

by

SUSAN BARRIE

Harlequin Books

TORONTO • LONDON • NEW YORK • AMSTERDAM
SYDNEY • HAMBURG • PARIS • STOCKHOLM

Original Hardcover edition published in 1956
by Mills & Boon Limited

ISBN 0-373-00628-4

Harlequin edition published November 1961
Second printing February 1967
Third printing March 1980

Printed in Canada

CHAPTER ONE

THE ROCKING and roaring of the train as it plunged headlong through the night was like something out of a nightmare to Karen, seated alone in a corner of her third-class compartment. It had been going on for so long, for one thing—it seemed an eternity since they had left King's Cross—and the lights in the compartment glowed like yellow eyes through the fog that had seeped in through a badly-fitting window after they passed through a tunnel, and induced a sensation of mascabre unreality. And as there was no one to exchange even a word with, and no one passed either up or down the corridor, which was a ribbon of gloom winding into nothingness, the slightly feverish conviction was taking root in her mind that there were no longer any other human beings in the world, and that this nightmare progress during which she could not snatch even a wink of sleep might go on for ever.

She shook her head to free it of this absurd conviction, but the feeling of unreality—the deathly weariness that was acting as fuel to her always rather vivid imagination—remained. It would not have been nearly so bad if she could have found one single comfortable spot on the padded back of the seat behind her against which she could rest her head, and having found it, closed her eyes and drifted, if only for a few minutes, into an uneasy slumber. But the back of the seat might have been made of iron so far as her head was concerned, and her whole body was so full of weariness that it was one continuous ache.

She supposed that this was only the normal result of undertaking a long journey almost immediately after coming out of hospital, and it would have been much more sensible if she had delayed this journey for another twenty-four hours at least. But her little two-roomed flat in the Bayswater district of London had struck her as so completely unhomelike, and there had been no one but her landlady to do anything at all for her—and that very grudgingly! She had felt she simply had to get away at once, and Nannie McBain had been the only person she could think of who would receive her with open arms.

Ever since she left King's Cross she had been thinking of Nannie, and the welcome that awaited her when she finally reached the end of her journey. Nannie—or Ellen—McBain had looked after her when she was very small. Her parents had been in a position to maintain quite a staff of servants in those days. At least, there had been a cook and a couple of housemaids, as well as the rosy-cheeked Scotswoman who had got married to one of her own countrymen shortly after Karen's seventh birthday, and gone away up into the far north of Scotland to live. And shortly after that Karen's father, whose interests were all bound up with the Stock Exchange, had made some sort of a wild plunge that had resulted in the family's fortunes being completely reversed, and they were no longer able to keep even one housemaid, let alone a cook. Karen had been sent away to school and therefore it had been unnecessary to replace Nannie McBain.

But more than one holiday had Karen spent with Ellen, and the two had kept in close touch, especially after an air disaster had deprived the girl of both parents. In the long and often lonely years devoted to the slow process of growing up and arriving at an age when she could be reasonably expected to take care of herself—and at twenty-three one certainly *ought* to be able to do that quite adequately, she thought a little wryly, as she sought to ease her position in the corner seat, and longed for the night to pass — she had been glad to know that there was Ellen, as solid and dependable as the

Rock of Gibralter, not too easily reached in her remote cottage, but definitely there if one needed her. She had been glad of Ellen's cards at Christmas time, and her parcels of home-made gingerbread and knitted undergarments on her birthdays, with a little loving note folded into the stout vests which were never worn. In hospital, while she made the feeblest efforts to throw off pneumonia (which she had incurred, she knew, because of her cowardly fear of her landlady, and her dislike of troubling her when she caught a bad bout of 'flu which had been consequently neglected, and she was lucky not to have departed this life altogether instead of being whisked into a white ward by a chance visitor who called to see her), her mind had clung to the thought of her old nurse like a drowning person clinging to a raft.

Ellen, in the small, grey stone cottage which was just one of several exactly similar cottages in the tiny village where she lived. Ellen's front room, which was so full of knick-knacks that one could hardly get into it, and which smelt a little of mothballs, although her kitchen always reeked superbly of the kind of cooking which should have won her a medal. And her tiny spare bedroom, with its snowy white counterpane on the deep feather bed, and the dressing-table standing in a kind of pink sateen petticoat, while the walls were almost entirely obscured by large, colorful prints. Karen felt sure that as soon as she was free to gratify her almost over-powering longing for something dear and familiar *that* was the one room in the one house in all the world where strength would flow back into her veins, and where, despite Nannies almost certain scolding because she had so stupidly allowed herself to get pneumonia, and have never worn the woolly vests which might have prevented it, she would soon be quite herself again.

So almost immediately she was discharged from the hospital she had sent a telegram to Ellen, whom she had neither seen nor heard from for several months, to announce that she was on her way, and had then packed a few things in a suitcase and set off for King's Cross.

But she had been hardly prepared for the wearisomness of this journey, and the fact that she was so far from well yet that it was almost an agony to her to have to sit upright for hours on end, because she could not afford a sleeper. The thought of stretching herself out at full length on a comfortable bed began to have the same effect on her as the thought of drinking cool water would have on a man dying of thirst in the desert, and the confusion of her mind was increased by the rattle and roar of the train.

But shortly before dawn she did manage to sink into a doze, and it was just as she was drifting into this doze that the recollection of the man who had come to her assistance at King's Cross passed vaguely across her brain, and she found herself wondering for a moment in which part of the train he was, and whether he was enjoying his sleeper.

For she was quite certain he was occupying a sleeper, and as a result of their brief acquaintance she was just as certain that it would be first-class. Very definitely he was the type of man who always travelled first, whether it was on a train or a boat or on an air liner—and from the vast quantity of luggage which accompanied him, heavily plastered with labels covering half the globe, or so it had seemed to her, and most of the cases made of pigskin or calf, he was most decidedly a traveller who really merited the title.

His taxi had come up behind her own when she had arrived at the station, and while an obsequious porter had attended to his luggage and she had fumbled in her purse for change for her own taxi fare he had glanced in an indifferent manner across at her. Perhaps because she looked young, and was not particularly smart, and the driver of her taxi eyed her doubtfully while she tried to make up her mind about the size of the tip he should receive—she was always a little afraid of under-tipping taximen, in case they should let her see their displeasure—no porter came hastening up to her to assist her with her luggage. Although it was only one suitcase, it was heavy, and while she was trying to struggle with it herself she managed somehow to drop her handbag; her purse fell out and a shower of coins cascaded from it and ran in all directions over the grey flags of the station yard.

She was bending in confusion to pick them up when the man with the mountain of baggage strolled quietly across to her and started to assist her; and at last, flushed and almost stammering with embarrassment, she managed to thank him for collecting most of the coins. She looked up at him as she offered her thanks. He seemed to be towering above her, and because it was a bitterly cold January evening the heavy duffel coat he was wearing struck her as the most highly suitable garb in the world. He was hatless, and his hair was very black, and in the harsh brilliance of the station lights she could see that his eyes were cool and grey. Something flickered in them for a moment as she tried to find words to express her appreciation, and when she thought about it afterwards she wondered whether it was amusement, or perhaps a mixture of amusement and surprise.

"I think that's the lot," he said, as he handed over several half-crowns and some smaller silver. "I don't think you've suffered any serious loss."

"No—no, I'm sure I haven't," she answered, and tried to smile at him shakily.

He bent to pick up her suitcase, which looked very shabby compared with the beautiful specimens of his own luggage, bulging at the seams as it was.

"Do you want a porter?" he asked, with a faintly raised eyebrow. "Or are you by any chance travelling on the same train as myself—the Night Scot? Because if you are I can put this into your carriage for you."

"Thank you, that—that would be kind," she told him, and realized that after the little excitement of rescuing her money and finding herself confronted by this tall stranger her breath was behaving erratically; in fact, it was coming very unevenly, and much too quickly for comfort. And although she did not know it, once the painful blush slid out of her cheeks it left her looking almost alarmingly pale by contrast, and she thought the man's eyes rested on her searchingly.

But he said nothing as they walked side by side towards the platform prescribed by the indicator, and once they reached the train he stopped beside the door of a first-class compartment.

"This do?" he asked, grasping the handle of the door.

But Karen quickly undeceived him.

"I'm travelling third," she said simply.

Again he said nothing, and they went on until they came upon a line of thirds. He put her into the empty compartment, her suitcase on the rack, and then stepped down again on to the platform. He looked up at her before he closed the door.

"All right?" he enquired.

"Perfectly all right, thank you," she managed, and watched him walk away briskly along the platform in the direction of his luggage and the porter who was carefully guarding his own seat for him.

But just before the rattle of the wheels faded from her consciousness, and the yellow lights in the compartment ceased to be yellow, watchful eyes, she had a brief, clear glimpse of his face, as if it had been photographed and placed directly in front of her, and there was nothing she could possibly miss about it. His hair had a slight wave above his left eyebrow, and it was sleek and shining like the plumage of a bird, and his features were wonderfully regular. He had very black eyelashes, too—almost feminine eyelashes. But there was nothing feminine about the gleam of the grey eyes behind them, and the set of his mouth and chin. His was the kind of chin that had nothing whatever to do with weakness.

She sighed, a queer little fluttering sigh that began life deep down inside her, and she said to herself that he was nice—nice and kind!

It would have been almost a physical impossibility for her to carry her own suitcase to the train, which showed how ridiculously weak she was!

CHAPTER TWO

LATE THE following afternoon she stood on an almost deserted platform at Inverlochie station and watched the few people who had alighted from the train disappearing through the barrier. There were one or two cars drawn up on the other side of the barrier, and beyond the cars a steep street wound upwards between neat houses and shops to the tower of a stoutly built church which lifted itself above the climbing roofs and soared in splendid isolation into the cold, sunset-flushed air.

This sunset light also bathed the purple wall of hills which ringed them in, and the dark woods clothing them in patches. The sky was clear, like a sea of tender turquoise, or an inverted blue lake across which very soon now the shadows would fall. With the falling of those shadows the cold would increase, and already it was intense enough to set Karen's teeth chattering almost uncontrollably as she gazed rather helplessly about her. She had a hollow, slightly sick feeling inside, for she had eaten practically nothing at all that day, and although when she arrived in Edinburgh that morning she could have breakfasted very comfortably she had made do with a cup of coffee because at that time she had not been inclined to bother with food. For some reason, although at times she felt extremely hungry, at others even the thought of forcing some solid substance past her lips filled her with nausea.

But now, after the warmth of the train, the long hours of sitting, and probably as a result of her empty interior, she was conscious of feeling so bewildered by the cold that her cramped limbs bent under her, and it was well-nigh impossible to prevent them from shivering. She tried to force herself to think clearly, telling herself that it would be impossible for her to reach Ellen that night, because the last bus which left for her village must have left already, and the only sensible thing was to find herself a hotel. There was almost certainly more than one hotel in Inverlochie, and at this season of the year they would not be full; one of them would be small and reasonable and provide her with a bed, at least, into which she could crawl as soon as she reached it, and in that way stop this dreadful shivering which was making her knees knock, and her teeth chatter harder than ever.

She saw the porter at the barrier looking towards her somewhat curiously, and she bent to pick up her suitcase, which somehow she had managed to persuade to leave the rack in her recent train compartment, and allow itself to be dumped on the platform. But now she couldn't get a grip of the handle, and in any case it was too heavy, and——

She heard a voice speaking to her, sharply, out of hazy clouds of bewilderment, and she thought she recognized a face as it wavered in front of her.

"Can I help you?" the voice asked. "Have you any idea at all where you're going?"

And then the voice ceased abruptly, and the man caught her as she sagged and swung her up into his arms, where at least she was no longer in any danger of falling. The porter, who had been collecting tickets, hurriedly deserted the barrier and joined him, and the two of them stood looking down at the limp form of the girl whose fair head dangled pathetically over the duffel-coated arm of the tall man who held her, her small, heart-shaped face absolutely colorless. It was a delicately-featured face—rather like a flower when color warmed it, although an exceptionally fragile flower at that—but now the soft lips were pinched and blue, and there were heavy purple smudges beneath the closed eyes. The porter, who had a daughter of his own about this young woman's age, gazed sympathetically, and then he said quickly:

"Come along with me, Mr. Mackenzie, sir, and we'll get her out of this cold wind. 'Tis like knives tearing into you, and I've no doubt at all it's from cold she's fainted."

But Iain Mackenzie was not so sure of that as he stood beside the hard horse-hair sofa on which his recent burden had been placed, in a somewhat dingy waiting-room where, however, a bright fire was blazing half-way up the chimney, and waited for her to show some signs of returning consciousness. He had managed to get a little brandy between her lips, and had vigorously chafed her hands and her small, ice-cold feet, but the waxen pallor of her face remained, and he felt a strange anxiety deep down inside him; a feeling of guilt, also, because the night before when she had struck him as being quite unfitted for travel at the late hour of the night he had done nothing about it, and asked her no questions.

And yet, on the other hand, what questions could he have asked her that she might not have resented? And what business was it of his, anyway?

Nevertheless, he caught his lower lip between his hard white teeth and gnawed at it thoroughly for several seconds while he continued to gaze at her, and his black brows met in an almost straight line above the noticeably high bridge of his nose. When the porter made his appearance with a steaming mug of hot tea he waved it away.

"Let's make another attempt to revive her with the brandy," he said, and held out a lean, commanding hand for it.

This time he succeeded in getting her to swallow some of the raw spirit, and within a matter of moments after that the faintest tinge of color stole into her cheeks and disipated some of that alarming pallor. Her long eyelashes lifted, and as he picked up one of her hands and held it strongly between both his own a pair of dull blue eyes—that reminded him of a blaze of blue larkspur seen through a misted window—gazed back into his own, and a thread-like voice enquired:

"What——what has happened?"

"It's all right," he assured her, as she attempted to struggle up into a sitting position. "You fainted when you got out of the train just now—I don't think you've eaten very much for a good many hours, have you?" with a shrewd, considering look at her. "But you'll feel better when you've got inside a little of this." He placed the cup of hot tea in her shaking hands, taking the precaution of keeping a firm grip of it with one of his own hands while she took a few uncertain sips. "Don't talk for a few moments, but try to drink as much as you can."

She obeyed him, lying back against the hard pillow of the horse-hair sofa, and thinking in a kind of vague wonderment how extraordinary it was that he should be the man who had apparently come to her rescue yet again! The man with the dark hair and the quiet grey eyes who travelled first, and who had wanted to put her into a first-class carriage also! The color increased in her cheeks, and as the combined effects of the hot tea and the brandy she had consumed drove away the last of the icy chill from her limbs, and a warm and comforting glow began to take its place, her eyes also started to glow a little, until the effect of a misty window was banished along with her pallor, and at the same time they were suddenly so acutely shy that she could hardly meet his look.

"I'm afraid I—it wasn't just because I—I haven't eaten very much," she told him truthfully, at last. "I've only just come out of hospital, and I don't think I was really fit to travel——"

"I'm quite sure you were not," he responded a little curtly.

The larkspur-blue eyes were suddenly heavy with wistfulness.

"But I'd only two rooms to go back to, and there was no one there even to talk to, and I thought of Nannie McBain. . . . I'm on my way to her now."

"What were you in hospital for?" he asked, even more curtly.

"I caught a bad dose of 'flu, and it turned into pneumonia." She smiled apologetically. "I'm sorry I'm such a nuisance, but I honestly thought I was much better than I am. Otherwise I'd have put up with the two rooms—only they're not really two rooms, only a bedroom and a kind of kitchenette."

"And who would have looked after you?" he wanted to know, with so much unmistakable grimness that she actually began to feel a little frightened of him all at once. "Why, I—I don't know. . . . My landlady might have done a little shopping for me, and she might even have cooked for me if I'd made it worth her while. But I'd have managed all right. It was just the loneliness that I didn't feel I could face, somehow." Her eyes pleaded with him, and they were clouded again with anxiety. "Can you tell me if I can find a room for tonight? A hotel room? I know it's no use trying to get to Nannie tonight—the last bus to Craigie will have gone, and I don't expect there are any taxis I can hire. There never are very many, and they're usually snapped up as soon as the train comes in. And, in any case,

I think I'll feel a little more like it in the morning—" swallowing something in her throat, because in spite of the fact that she was completely revived, the thought of the effort it would require to get herself off the couch and outside to a hotel was somehow in itself a little appalling. And she didn't want to do anything silly again, like fainting right under this man's eyes, and putting him to the trouble of bringing her round with brandy which he had undoubtedly had to purchase, and cups of hot tea.

She put down the empty cup she was holding on a convenient little table beside her, and made a determined effort to rise, but he said quickly, before she could slide one foot to the ground:

"Stay where you are, and we'll get things sorted out in a moment." He walked to the uncurtained window and stood looking out at the now completely deserted platform, glowing with the last angry redness of the sunset, while around there was a feeling of night, dark and inpenetrable, waiting to swoop upon them at any moment. Through the partly open doorway of the waiting-room the cold found its way in, like an almost tangible thing, and Karen began to shiver on the couch, realizing that in about another hour it would almost certainly be freezing. How unwise she had been even to think about coming north at this season of the year, when she was physically such a poor thing, and even her best tweed coat had not enough substance to combat the rigors of this sort of weather!

From the window the man's voice reached her.

"Craigie?" he echoed. "You want to get to Craigie, and you mentioned a Nannie McBain. Is that Ellen McBain?"

"Yes." She turned her head over her shoulder, and tried to get a glimpse of his face. "D-do you know her?" half hopefully.

"Yes; I know her quite well, and what's more I can take you to her tonight. I've a car outside."

"But——" in spite of the sudden relief, a disturbing thought assailed her. Supposing—just supposing Ellen had not received her telegram, or for some reason was away from home! What a dreadful thing that would be!—"But won't it be causing you a lot of inconvenience?" There was no doubt about the anxiety in her eyes, because she knew she *was* causing him inconvenience, as he turned and walked back to her and met them with his slightly inscrutable grey ones. "I'm already holding you up——"

"Not at all," he answered, his tone as uncommunicative as his looks, although when she had first recovered consciousness after that extraordinary faint there had been nothing but gentleness in his expression, which she was not likely to forget. "I've got to go through Craigie, and I can drop you off there." He smiled at her suddenly, a rather odd smile. "By the way, I'd better introduce myself, hadn't I?" I'm Iain Mackenzie."

"And I'm Karen March."

She said it in the shy voice he was beginning to associate with her, and his smile softened a little, so that all at once it was extremely attractive.

"Well, Miss March, I'll be happier about you when I know you're handed over to somebody who can really look after you, and as it won't do you any good to remain here in this draughty waiting-room we'll get outside to the car, shall we?" As she made an instant movement to rise he prevented her by slipping one hand expertly under her slim knees, and another behind her back, and lifting her—as he had lifted her once before, barely a quarter of an hour before—right into his arms. And, ignoring her protestations that she was quite capable of walking, he carried her outside to his car.

And what a car it was, she decided, when she first caught sight of it in the rapidly failing light. Entirely in keeping with his pigskin suitcases, and the aura of opulence which clung to him. Low-slung, black and glistening, with a chauffeur seated behind the wheel, who jumped out immediately and greeted his master with obvious pleasure, while at the same time apparently accepting it as normal that he should be carrying a young woman in his arms. Unless he had been previously warned by the porter!

Karen gave a sigh of exquisite relief when she found herself lying back against the silvery-grey upholstery, and the comfort of the superbly sprung seat was beneath her weary body. To be able to rest her head against yielding cushions was almost too much for her just then, and as Iain Mackenzie got in beside her and tucked a rug over her knees and closed the door she shut her eyes tightly, because of the rush of relieved tears under her too-white eyelids.

It was quite dark by the time they sped through Craigie, and there were scarcely any lights in the windows of the cottages fringing the main street. The simple front of Ellen McBain's cottage, with its small windows heavily festooned with lace curtaining, and shining brass knocker on the front door, was in absolute blackness, and the car did not even hesitate for a moment as it swept on its way up the slight incline at the summit of which the open country began once more. But as she was by this time sunk in entirely peaceful sleep, Karen had no idea of what was happening around her.

And she had only a confused impression, when she was later carried from the car and handed over to someone else, of bright lights which hurt her eyes and voices which murmured without her understanding in the least what they were murmuring about. And as the sleep which drugged her was too deep and too persistent to be thrown off for more than a moment, even those lights and those voices were quickly lost to her, and the blissful moment when something like a floating cloud received her, and a delicious warmth stole all about her, brought nothing more than the faintest of smiles to her lips, and she sighed—a long, shuddering sigh of relief. And then she went on sleeping.

CHAPTER THREE

OUTSIDE IT WAS one of those days when the very air sparkled, and the sky was a clear, cold blue. There was a resinous smell in the air, too, from the forests of larch and juniper which clothed the gaunt hill-sides, and the sunlight picked out all the colors in the distant mountain tops. At one moment they were a tawny gold, and then they were emerald overlaid with violent patches of purple. When the sun re-treated behind a cloud for a moment the purple pre-dominated, and they looked sullen and brooding peaks, thrusting their shoulders against that hard backcloth of sky. But the instant the sun reappeared all the little half-frozen cascades finding their way down into the valleys stared to gleam like silver ribbons, and the constant gurgle of running water echoed amongst the leafless woods that surrounded Craigie House.

From her large four-poster bed, Karen could see out of the big bay window and away across the tops of trees to that superb view of Scottish mountains. They awed her because she had never seen moun-tains more impressive, and their brooding beauty on such a morning as this was something that did strange things to her internally, and filled her with a queer kind of humility, because by comparison she was so completely inadequate and, as she felt at that moment, colorless.

It was true that about her shoulders there was a fleecy pink bed-jacket that lent just a touch of color to her cheeks, and her short-curling hair had a ribbon looped through it that kept it out of her eyes, and the ribbon was pink, also. Mrs. Burns, who had been housekeeper at Craigie House for more years than she cared to remember sometimes, had discovered the ribbon amongst the contents of Karen's suitcase, and because she thought the girl needed something to brighten up her appearance she had fastened it into the fair hair.

Mrs. Burns was an extraordinarily comfortable person to have about one, and although she was extremely efficient, it was the kind of efficiency that was kept well hidden by a soothing manner. She never bustled into a room, or appeared to have little time to spare, or disdained gossip. She always seized the opportunity to sink into a chair by Karen's bed and discuss the shortcomings of the various maids without any rancor or serious disapproval in her voice. She also told Karen bluntly that she had a long way to go before she was completely fit, and that she would have to take great care of herself in the future. Dr. Robert Moffat, from the village, had uttered strongly disapproving noises after he had been afforded an opportunity to examine Karen's chest, and the warning he had passed on to Mrs. Burns was that unless the girl was looked after and kept warm and snug in bed for several days, and watched closely after that, he would prefer not to be the one who was responsible for her.

So Mrs. Burns kept enormous fires going in Karen's room, and they blazed half-way up the chimney, looking immensely attractive framed in the white garlanded fireplace. At night, the flames leapt and played on the pastel-tinted walls of the room, and the white paintwork glistened and shone in the mellow glow of lamplight which streamed from the bedside table. The deep pink eiderdown on the enormous bed looked fat and opulent, the bed-curtains, although they were drawn back, were cosily pink also, and the carpet which covered every inch of the floor was a kind of warm claret color which turned to cardinal red when the embers blazed at their hottest.

Karen had hot-water bottles at her feet, and on each side of her, so that she sometimes felt she was being a little bit smothered by over-kindness, but rather than let Mrs. Burns guess this she endured the discomfort with fortified special meals were prepared for her in the kitchen of Craigie House that would have set her mouth watering under normal conditions, but with very little appetite she had to struggle to do justice to them because Mrs. Burns was bent on "building her up." To keep her company Mrs. Burns brought her knitting and sat with her in the evenings, while the wind sometimes howled about the house in the frozen night outside, and the threat of snow came close, and then receded—for as yet, apparently, there had been none.

"But we'll get it before long now—you mark my words!" Mrs. Burns voiced it as her opinion, as she rocked herself lazily in the old-fashioned rocking chair which was her favorite, and seemed to rejoice in the direness of her own predictions. "And when it comes it'l no' be leaving us very soon! We're like to be snowed up here for a month and more, and like as not we'll be cut off from the village. I've known that happen many a time in the past, and that's why I never let my store cupboard get low. If the worst comes to the worst the one thing we'll not do is starve."

Karen watched her fascinated as her busy knitting-needles clicked away, and a look of the utmost complacency came over her face; and when she started to talk more thankfully about the master being safely at home for once, and not wandering about the world as he had been strangely tempted to do for the past year and more, Karen pricked up her ears a little because, although she had been at Craigie House now for nearly a week, she had not once set eyes on her host since that night when she had fainted in his arms at Inverlochie.

When she had first discovered where she was she had been utterly confused and bewildered.

"But why am I here and not at Nannie McBain's?" she had asked Mrs. Burns.

"If you mean Ellen McBain," the housekeeper had answered, "she's away to look after her brother who's sick, and as he's sick in Aberdeen she could scarcely be looking after you at the same time. No, you're far better here at Craigie House, believe me, and here you'll have to make up your mind to stop until you're a great deal stronger than you are at present."

"But—but that's taking too great an advantage of your kindness!" Karen looked, and was, very much concerned, feeling that she had no right to be where she was. "It's inflicting myself on you."

Mrs. Burns gave her rather an odd look, but she exclaimed at once:

"What rubbish you're talking, my dear, and it's no trouble at all to look after you. You're as easy a patient as ever I've dealt with, and if you think that Mr. Mackenzie would be wishing you to go elsewhere——"

"But I came up to stay with Nannie, and as she isn't here I ought to go home!"

"And where," Mrs. Burns enquired, looking slightly ominous and sitting down beside her, "is home?"

Karen looked vaguely uncomfortable, and much less vaguely, disturbed.

"It's a little—a little flat I have in London——"

"And who, may I ask, would be looking after you there?"

"No one," Karen admitted. "But," she added stubbornly, "I could look after myself."

"Oh, aye," Mrs. Burns agreed with her there, in a tone of heavy sarcasm, "we've seen something of your looking after yourself, and what it resulted in. One dose of pneumonia, and you were heading straight for another, if Mr. Iain hadn't had the sound commonsense to bring you straight here, and not even to waste any time knocking up Ellen McBain! And a waste of time it would have been, for she's been gone from her house for nearly a fortnight."

"Then she never even got my telegram," Karen murmured, wondering a little wistfully whether Ellen ever would receive that telegram, and if she did whether she would get in touch with her. For, kind as Mrs. Burns was, and luxurious as were her present surroundings, there is a feeling of security in having someone in connection with whom one can claim some sort of belonging, and Ellen had never failed her before. In addition to which there was a natural shrinking in Karen's breast from accepting anything in the nature of charity from anyone, especially complete strangers.

"Oh, as to the telegram," Mrs. Burns replied to that, " 'tis more than likely it'll be waiting for Ellen on her front door mat when she returns, and by that time you'll be feeling more like your old self. So I wouldn't worry about that."

But Karen did worry, while accepting with apparent meekness the ministrations of people about her, and feeling at the same time whole-heartedly grateful for so much unstinted kindness. If only she could get rid of the feeling that somewhere in the house Iain Mackenzie, with his penetrating grey eyes and quiet speech, and that unostentatiously capable way of his of dealing with an emergency, was looking with annoyance upon this invasion of his home.

However humane he was, however much she had succeeded in arousing his pity, at least there were limits to the amount of consideration one should display towards a stranger. And if she had chosen any other moment to collapse in a dead faint than the one when he was checking his luggage as it was carried off the train at Inverlochie, their paths would never have become entwined like this.

As a result of discreet enquiries she had already elicited the information that he was a bachelor, and that this was a bachelor's household. And a sick girl thrown upon the kind-heartedness of a bachelor could become a serious embarrassment to him.

The odd part about it was that Mrs. Burns did not seem to look upon it in that way. She persisted in regarding Karen as more or less a normal guest who had had the misfortune to be taken ill in the house, and negatived every protest made by Karen that she was causing trouble.

"Mr. Mackenzie would be the last to admit that you're any trouble, my dear," she said to her more than once. And then added, somewhat surprisingly: "But you know that, don't you?"

One morning, when Karen had occupied her delightful bedroom for about a week, and the doctor had cut down his daily visits to every other day, Mrs. Burns came bustling into the room, and told Karen that she was to be permitted to get up for a short while.

"Just in your dressing-gown, and to sit beside the window for a wee while, if you'd like to," she told her. She took Karen's dressing-gown out of the commodious wardrobe and helped her into it, fastening the girdle securely about her waist, and placing a camel-hair rug over her knees when she was ensconced in her chair by the window. The dressing-gown was a faded blue, and it had the effect of heightening Karen's fragile appearance almost alarmingly, but her fair hair caught all the sunshine, and looked like a nimbus framing her face. She watched in faint surprise as the housekeeper made a few rapid movements about the room tidying this and straightening that, and when a knock came on the door and Mrs. Burns flew to open it her surprise increased. And then her heart did a most peculiar bound under the faded dressing-gown, and she found herself gripping the arms of her chair. Color rushed up over her face, and for a few seconds after that she looked as if there was nothing very much wrong with her, for outside in the thickly carpeted corridor stood the tall figure of her host, looking as if he had just come in from a brisk walk in the invigorating air outside, with a bright, alert gleam in his eyes, and a healthy, rugged color under his deeply tanned skin.

Not only did he look as if he had been recently taking exercise in that attractive, half-frozen world beyond the windows, but he brought that faintly resinous smell of the woods with him. As he stepped inside the room, after hesitating for only a moment while Mrs. Burns openly beamed at him, he looked about him for a moment in slight curiosity, as if he was unfamiliar with this particular wing of his house, sent a quick glance towards Karen who was still clutching the arms of her chair, and then looked inquiringly at Mrs. Burns.

"I haven't arrived at an inconvenient moment? You haven't been putting the patient into a flutter getting her ready to receive me?"

His tone was jocular, but his eyes were keen as they bored their way into the housekeeper's face. She answered at once, as she prepared to slip past him and out into the corridor.

"Of course not, Mr. Iain! And, as a matter of fact, I think it's high time Miss March saw someone apart from myself to cheer her up a bit." Her smiling look roved between the two of them. "But remember this is the first time she's been out of bed for a week, and I can't allow you more than a quarter of an hour or so."

With this injunction she left the room, and the door closed behind her. Karen supposed it was because she was so ridiculously weak, but every pulse in her body seemed to be fluttering nervously, and her confusion showed in her eyes. This morning they were very blue, but they were also unnaturally large, and the pupils themselves looked dark and distended. Her long eyelashes seemed to be lightly dusted with gold dust at the tips, and they wavered uncertainly as he moved across the room and stood beside her.

His smile was curious, enigmatic. His eyes dwelt on her thoughtfully, making no attempt to conceal the fact that he was deliberately studying her, and they were the cool, detached grey eyes she remembered, under the almost feminine eyelashes. But how exceedingly masculine he seemed this morning, and by comparison with herself how one-hundred-per-cent fit. And it was obvious that his tailor knew how to make the most of his lithe, graceful proportions. His shoulders were broad, but not too broad; his hips were narrow, and she imagined he would look at his best in a kilt, and at his very best in Highland evening dress. But even in tweeds, faultlessly made as they were, there was something about him which set him apart from any other man she had ever met before. He wore a silk shirt and a flowing tie that was the badge of a well-known public school, and Karen became distressfully aware of her shabby dressing-gown that was not even particularly durable any longer, as she felt that his eyes flickered over it.

"Well," he asked, "how are you?" and the kindness in his voice was, she thought, carefully introduced into it. There was just the right amount of kindness, and no more. If her appearance affected him with any concern it was barely noticeable in his expression as he stood gazing down at her.

Karen made a little, rather helpless movement with one of her hands. She did not answer his question, but said huskily:

"Why didn't you stop at Nannie McBain's that night you brought me here? You didn't, did you?"

"Didn't I?" For an instant he looked genuinely amused, and he took a seat on the arm of a chair and continued to study her. "Perhaps I thought it would be a waste of time, and it was important to get you into a warm bed with as little delay as possible."

"But you couldn't have known Nannie was away from home—you'd been abroad and you'd only just returned! You brought me straight here."

"Which was plainly a very sensible thing to do, because your Nannie's house was empty, and still is, and I was quite sure Mrs. Burns could take charge of you just as adequately as Mrs. McBain."

"But that isn't the point." Her voice was even more husky, but she was determined to get this matter off her chest and dealt with without allowing herself to be side-tracked. "Don't you see that you've put me under an obligation? I mean, Nannie might have been there, and she might have got my telegram, and—and——"

"But she wasn't, and she didn't, and you are here!" he replied with a soft, smooth note in his voice. "Aren't you comfortable? Is there anything you feel that you lack? Because you have only to tell Mrs. Burns."

"Of course not," she exclaimed, a little impatiently. And then as she saw him remove his cigarette case from his pocket and then tuck it hastily back again she said more naturally: "It's quite all right for you to smoke, for I'm hardly coughing at all now. In fact, I'm so much better that I feel I oughn't to allow myself to be waited on as I am being. I feel a bit of a fraud."

"Do you?" Iain Mackenzie murmured, but this time both his voice and his look were gentle. It was a gentleness that brought a faint flush to her cheeks.

"And I'm being a nuisance, too. I'm giving you a lot of trouble," she went on.

CHAPTER FOUR

HE DID NOT TAKE advantage of her permission to smoke, but stood up and wandered to the window and stood looking out at the view, which was obviously one of his favorites.

"In a few weeks from now," he told her, "there will be nothing but a sea of young green foliage and green shoots everywhere to be seen from this window. But the mountains are pretty much the same all the year round. Smiling one minute, and frowning the next. This morning, because it's your first time up, they're smiling at you."

"But Mrs. Burns says there's plenty of time for snow yet," she told him, rather sombrely. "In fact, she's expecting it. She's expecting Craigie to be cut off by snow."

He turned with a kind of half smile.

"Oh, Mrs. Burns!—— She loves to be a little dramatic. But does the thought of being imprisoned in Craigie by snow fill you with any sort of alarm?"

"No." She shook her head to emphasize the negative, but she met his eyes squarely at the same time. "However, I mustn't think of remaining here for much longer, must I? I've already inflicted myself on you for a week, and that was something you never expected when you met me for the first time outside King's Cross station."

"Maybe not," he agreed, dropping down on to the cushioned window-ledge and thrusting his hands into his pockets. "But talking of King's Cross station—how often have you visited Craigie before? And when was the last time you were here?"

"Oh, not for several years." Her eyes smiled a wistfully, a little reminiscently, as she recalled that last occasion. "But I've always loved it, and thought it the most enchanting spot in the world. But the odd thing is," gazing at him in perplexity, "that I don't remember ever seeing or hearing of Craigie House before. If Nannie mentioned it—and she must have done — it left no impression on my mind. Perhaps that's because you were not living here at the time. I'm quite sure I would have remembered you if I'd seen you, even if I was only small"—looking faintly abashed because his eyes became amused—"or I'd have been puzzled by a likliness—"

"I don't really think that's very likely," he answered, the amusement in his voice as well. "One has to allow for the fact that when you were last here there were still a good many years between us, and we do alter as we grow older, you know. And, in any case, my family were not very addicted to Craigie in the first flush of my own youth, and we only came here for holidays as a rule."

She looked about her at the large room, with its garlanded ceiling, its wide white fireplace, and other graceful features.

"It's beautiful," she said, still more wistfully. "I can't imagine anyone not wanting to live here."

"I always think that when I come back to it after an absence," he admitted. "Especially after a prolonged absence."

There was silence for a few moments, and then he leaned a little towards her, his hands removed from his pockets and clasped between his knees.

"I haven't bothered you before this because I thought you'd rather be left alone with Mrs. Burns until you felt stronger. But I do want to have a little talk with you about—yourself!"

He sensed rather than observed her instant reaction to this—something inside her tensing itself, becoming taut and anxious, perhaps a little on the defensive.

"Y-yes?" she stammered.

Mackenzie's smile at her was intended to do away with that tension and enable her to relax.

"You do realize that you were heading straight for pneumonia again that night when you arrived at Inverlochie?"

She nodded, and swallowed something in her throat.

"The doctor seemed to think I should have had a second dose of it."

"And old Moffat knows what he's talking about. He's a good doctor. One of the best. And he thinks you've got to be handled very carefully."

"But that's absurd"—she felt herself flushing painfully—"quite absurd. I'm not really in the least delicate, only I happened to neglect a chill, and that sort of thing happens to lots of people. It's the time of year when one develops chills, and I can't wrap myself up in cotton wool."

"But until you're a little bit stronger, at least, someone will have to wrap you up in cotton wool, or a repeat performance of what happened to you at Inverlochie is almost certain to follow—according to old Moffat!"

The blush burned like fire in her cheeks.

"You mean, I—I'll make myself a nuisance to other people?"

"Well," with an odd smile, "you can't very well make a practice of fainting in the arms of unknown males, can you? For one thing, they may not always be provided with a car, or a convenient house to which they can take you, and the consequences could be disastrous for you. I think if it's humanly possible we must avoid any possibility of the Inverlochie incident repeating itself in your case."

"But I—I have to earn my own living." Her voice was wavering now, and the distress in her eyes was unmistakable. "When Nannie comes back, I know she'll have me for a week or two, and then I can go back to London and get another job, if my old firm won't have me back. But I have *got* to work to keep myself!"

Iain Mackenzie stared at her in a hard and embarrassing fashion for what seemed to her a painfully long period of time.

"Have you?" he said slowly, at last. "Well, we'll see!" He got up and started to pace about the room, and then came back to her. "I've been in touch with your Nannie McBain, and I might as well tell you now that there isn't the remotest hope that she'll be back at her cottage under a month, at least. She's nursing a relative whom she apparently can't leave, and although she's distressed about you there's nothing very much she can do to help."

"Oh!" Karen exclaimed faintly.

"So I'm afraid you'll have to make up your mind to stay here. It's the only thing you can do."

"But that's impossible!" She sat up very straight in her chair, and once again she gripped the arms of it. "Oh, don't you see," she appealed to him, "I can't possibly go on forcing myself on you like this? For one thing it isn't fair, and——"

"You don't find it very comfortable?"

"Of course it's comfortable—it's wonderfully comfortable! But it isn't even as if—as if you were—I mean, you're not even—not even——"

"Married?"

The confusion in her face answered him.

"That's quite true," he agreed, starting his leisurely pacing up and down again, "and this is a strictly bachelor household. But I got over that difficulty at the beginning by telling Mrs. Burns—who no doubt passed it on to all her underlings!—that you and I were thinking about marrying one another, and that's why I brought you north! I didn't even let her know that we met for the first time in the process of catching a north-bound train, and if you've unwisely informed her otherwise then it can't be helped, but there's all the more reason why we should stick to my early tale and pretend, for the time being, at least, that we're engaged. It won't do you any harm to put up a little pretence, and if you don't I shall have to think up some excuse for leaving home again fairly soon, and that won't benefit you at all because you'll probably think up some plan for running away also, and back you'll be in further trouble. So what do you say?"

Karen was unable to say anything for a few moments, and she was not quite certain whether a return of light-headedness was causing her to imagine things, or whether he was indeed in earnest. In the end the absolute coolness of his look as it bored into her convinced her that that was just what he was—coolly and calmly in earnest!

"But—but——"

"Do you realize that I've been away from home for over a year, wandering, as my old aunt puts it, 'about the globe,' and it's a little upsetting to my plans to have to think about finding other accommodation just now? So what do you say?"

"I don't know what to say," she confessed weakly. "I've never heard anything so—so——"

"Don't say it," he urged her. "It's not in the least fantastic really—it's merely expedient. A remedy for a difficult situation which we've got to face up to. In a few weeks you'll probably be so fit that you'll be able to say goodbye to me with equanimity, but at present you're so very far from fit that it doesn't seem to me you have any choice in the matter."

"I could go into hospital," she whispered. "The doctor could get me into hospital."

"He could," Iain agreed, "but he would probably think it strange to be requested to do that when I've already told him you're my fiancée, and Craigie has any number of empty bedrooms!"

After that he was almost shocked by the sudden whiteness of her face, the bewildered look in her eyes, and he paused and bent over her and put his hand on her shoulder for a moment.

"Look," he said gently, "you don't have to make any decision about this today. But have you told Mrs. Burns anything at all about yourself?"

"Only that I expected to stay with Nannie McBain."

"Well, that's perfectly all right. She knows Nannie McBain, and you would probably have preferred to stay with her. Mrs. Burns will understand that. It's perfectly natural."

"But you musn't even think about leaving your own home just because of me! It would be dreadful if you had to do that——" with an appalled quiver in her voice.

"Don't worry about that." He patted her shoulder lightly, and Karen was amazed at the sudden softening of his face, the compassion in the grey eyes. "I'm not proposing to leave it today, anyway, and the important thing at the moment is to get you back to bed. I'm going to call Mrs. Burns, and tomorrow, if you feel like it, we'll have another talk. But in the meantime don't worry about anything."

Before the next day dawned, however, the cold brilliance of the weather had passed, and by evening there were leaden skies and a bleak north wind was blowing. Before Karen opened her eyes in the morning the soft, feathery flakes were fluttering down, and by the time she was sitting up in bed with a breakfast tray resting comfortably on her lap it was a white world outside. It was also a grey and ominous world, with the howling of the blizzard making a constant noise in her chimney. And when the wind dropped the snow simply continued to fall until every sound outside the windows was muffled by it.

Mrs. Burns was almost triumphant when she drew back Karen's curtains and let her see what was happening, and had happened, outside.

"I told you, didn't I?" she said. "And I'm never wrong! The snow's late this year, but it means business unless I'm no a weather prophet at all!"

Karen, from amidst her piled-up, lace-trimmed, feather pillows, gazed fascinatedly out the whirlwind of drifting white particles, and hardly knew whether to be concerned by what she saw or not. If this weather continued there was certainly no hope of her getting away from Craigie—there was no hope of anyone's getting away from Craigie!—and the situation inside the house would be extremely odd. She and her host would be pinned here together for weeks perhaps, and Mrs. Burns and the household staff already believed that they were contemplating marrying one another!

What an altogether absurd thought, Karen decided but she toyed with it for a moment as if it fascinated her. Two people who had not even known of one another's existence a week ago talking of becoming husband and wife, and pretending to be engaged for the sake of satisfying the proprieties.

But evidently Iain Mackenzie had firmly made up his mind that the proprieties would have to be satisfied—and he had done that before there had been any danger of being snowed up! How would he feel about the necessity for such a pretence after they had been cooped up together for weeks?

CHAPTER FIVE

It was once more a morning when the sky was blue and the sun shone, but the atmosphere was no longer freezingly cold, and there was even a certain softness—like a far-away breath of spring—in the air.

Most of the snow had vanished, save where the drifts had been tremendously deep, and where it still clung to the roofs of outhouses and stable buildings, and lay powdered and unbroken in the deep shade of the woods. But the roads were free and open once more, and Craigie House was no longer an entity entirely separate and cut off from the village of Craigie.

In the drawing-room of Craigie House Karen watched from the window a robin adventuring along the window sill outside, and she was certain the starry cluster of aconites in the bed outside the window had not been lifting up their faces to the friendly kiss of the sunshine the day before. There were some snowdrops in a vase near to her, too, which gave off a delicate fragrance, and these had been brought in from the shrubbery by Mrs. Burns, who had declared that they were actually forcing their way through what remained of the snow.

Karen lifted the window and scattered a few crumbs on the ledge for the robin, who had the courage to remain where he was and not to fly off while this operation was in progress, and then as she closed the window again she heard the door behind her open.

It was her host who had come into the room, and as always he seemed to bring a breath of the out-of-doors with him. Karen, as she turned back to the fire and met his eyes, had the feeling she so often had nowadays, and against which she was beginning to rebel, that she had become a kind of hot-house plant ridiculously guarded against the rigors of the outer air, and as she met those cool, alert eyes of Iain Mackenzie's, and saw the healthy glow which exercise had brought to his bronzed skin, a faint feeling of envy stirred in her, and the rebellion grew.

He had been walking down beside the lake, which he said was now free from ice, and he went to a cabinet, brought out a decanter and glasses and poured her a glass of sherry which he handed to her.

"Your very good health!" he said, a trifle mockingly she thought, as he raised his own glass. "If this weather continues you should be able to put your nose out of doors before very long, and then no doubt we shall see you begin to look positively robust. At the moment you certainly haven't enough color!"

She moved nearer to the fireplace and stood looking down into the glowing coals. She looked very slender as she stood there in her dress of fine grey wool, with a neat white collar and cuffs which lent it rather a Puritan touch. Her fair hair had grown a little longer, and was turning softly upwards on her neck like the petals of a flower, and her skin looked peculiarly flawless. Her mouth drooped a little despondently, but it was a very lovely mouth, especially as it was lightly lipsticked. She had a faint upward tilt to her small nose, too, which was also flower-like, and her long eyelashes fluttered noticeably as she stared at the fire.

"You know," she said suddenly, her untouched glass of sherry gripped tightly in one hand, "this is all quite ridiculous!"

"Oh!" Iain exclaimed. He flung himself comfortably into his favorite chair, and started to feel in all his pockets for his always elusive pipe and box of matches. "What is quite ridiculous?"

"Keeping me shut up like this, as if I were a—a precious plant, or something!" She flung back her head and looked at him, and her eyes were both hostile and accusing. "You know very well that it's got to end sometime and as I've already been here several weeks the sooner it ends the better! I can't go on living like this—accepting your charity—your — your goodness! You've been very kind, but——"

"Doctor's orders," he murmured imperturbably, as he started to stuff tobacco into the bowl of the pipe.

"Nonsense!" she exclaimed impatiently. "If Dr. Moffat knew the truth I'm quite sure he'd think you were eccentric!"

"Instead of which he thinks I'm contemplating marrying you and living happily ever after!"

There was so much faintly derisive amusement in his grey eyes as he looked up at her that she felt that revealing color, over which she had so little control, sting her cheeks, and for an instant she could not meet his eyes.

"If he thinks that it's simply because you—because we had to practice a deception. But I hate deception, and I hate deceiving anyone like Dr. Moffat. He's so kind, and so nice. And I don't like deceiving Mrs. Burns, either, or all the other people in this house."

"There's only the cook, and Annie," he reminded her. "Oh, and Prout, the parlormaid, and George, who drives my car. I shouldn't think the news has got as far as the village yet, as we've been cut off for so long. But Annie may carry it there when she goes in to change her library book at the village stores. They're served by a kind of travelling library service there, and——"

She gave a kind of exasperated sigh which caused his eyes to twinkle under his long and very thick black eyelashes as he bent over the bowl of his pipe.

"I don't really believe you mind," she said, staring at him in perplexity.

"Quite honestly, I don't," he answered, and having got the pipe to work satisfactorily lay back and sent a cloud of the fragrant tobacco smoke moving stealthily in her direction.

Karen gazed at him with her large eyes—still too large for her small, wan face—trying to solve the enigma of his bland, untroubled countenance. And as she gazed at him she could hardly believe that for nearly a month now they had been almost constant companions, sharing the faded splendors of this quiet room, with its pale green panelled walls and its gilded cornices, its mixture of period furniture and the portraits looking at them from the walls.

This room had been untouched for many years because it was lovely enough as it was, and there were no modern improvements that could make it more restful, or give it a greater charm. Karen had grown so accustomed to spending her evenings sitting on one side of the wide hearth while her host lounged on the other that she knew it was going to take a considerable effort to free her mind of the clinging memory of it. The memory of the damask-covered settees, and the long curtains falling before the windows, a rather deeper green than the walls, and of heavy brocade. The memory of the harp standing a little forlornly in one corner, and the piano at which Iain Mackenzie sometimes sat and amused himself—and her—with light syncopation, while the firelight played on the panelled walls, and the dusk deepened around them. The memory of a beautiful set of carved ivory chessmen, and an elegant chess board, which he brought out sometimes and set up on a small table between them; and the way in which, while he painstakingly taught her, who had never played chess before, to beat him at the game, the light from the standard lamp at his elbow discovering burnished gleams in his surprisingly black hair, while outside the snow lay hard and cold under a hard, cold moon.

When she left Craigie House she would have many memories to take away with her, and so many of them would be pleasant memories. But in the case of Iain Mackenzie these weeks of close confinement to the house and the society of a sickly young woman who had foisted herself upon him must have been weeks of pure, unalloyed boredom. Caught up in a ridiculous situation which, while it might sometimes have amused him a little, must at other times have irked him extremely, she could not understand how he so successfully turned to her an undisturbed front whenever she challenged him on the subject of their extraordinary intimacy.

For it was one thing to pretend to having acquired a fiancée in front of servants, but to have to keep up that pretence while day after day the snow fell steadily, the drifts which blocked the roads grew deeper, and the wireless was their only contact with the outer world, had aroused her own sympathy to such an extent that she was amazed that he did not seem either to require or desire to have it poured out over him.

Day after day his attitude towards her had remained the same — polite, attentive, considerate, even friendly. They had had many conversations, discussed all sorts of subjects, books, plays, even politics, but at the end of four weeks she was quite certain that neither of them really knew anything more of the other than when they first met. Perhaps it was because she was always on the defensive, while in him she always sensed, or imagined, that faint feeling of amusement—or derision, almost—which never allowed her to be quite at her ease (a thing which, under the circumstances, she could scarcely expect to be, as she realized) and which baffled her so much that he remained a stranger to her, in spite of the fact that the little world inside

Craigie House accepted him as the man she was going to marry. Whatever the reason, she felt that the four weeks had got them nowhere as regards looking into one another's minds.

And now he calmly informed her that he quite honestly didn't mind this situation, which she knew would have to end soon unless it was to become quite intolerable.

"Perhaps you'd like to read this," he said, removing an envelope from his pocket and tossing it lightly across to her. "It might provide you with a few ideas."

Karen seated herself in her customary armchair, and drew out the thick sheet of notepaper the envelope contained. She was so surprised that he had asked her to read part of his correspondence that she resitated before attempting to peruse the bold and yet rather spidery handwriting. It was a woman's writing, and the notepaper was that of a well-known and very exclusive London hotel. The letter, short and to the point, ran:

"Dear Nephew,

Delighted to hear your news, and anxious meet girl. Shall be returning Craigie the instant the snow clears, and then you'll be seeing me. Fiona has agreed to stay with me for a while—met her in Italy.

Your loving Aunt Horry."

Karen lifted her eyes from the letter and looked in bewilderment at her host.

"But—but I don't understand," she said.

Iain smiled.

"Well, I'll explain," he answered, "if you haven't already deduced the important point about that letter. Aunt Horry—my Aunt Horatia, that is, who was named after Nelson—has been spending part of the winter abroad, but as usual she's returned just at the wrong time, and within a matter of days she'll be lunching here in this house, unless I make a grave mistake. I wrote Aunt Horry in Italy—because she was already threatening a return—about you, and she seems to be quite charmed by the notion of acquiring a niece by marriage. I happen to be one of her favorite nephews, and she's always wanted me to marry. She has a house the other side of Craigie village, and once installed there again she'll be a frequent visitor, and you'll certainly have to get to know her. So you can't talk about running out on me just now, even if you were fit to do so, which you aren't yet."

"But—" she almost gaped at him—"you don't *really* mean to tell me that you told your own relative we were engaged?"

"I do," with amusement gleaming in his eyes.

"And who," she asked, after drawing a deep breath, " is Fiona?"

This time the expression on his face altered, and grew hard and cold all at once—so hard, and so cold, that for just a few moments she felt that he was almost a complete stranger to her.

"She and I were once really engaged," he explained, in, however, an absolutely level tone, "and then she decided to drop me in favor of an old friend of mine. The marriage only lasted a couple of years, and now she's a widow. Aunt Horry seems to have run across her in Italy and she's bringing her back with her—for some mysterious reason known only to Aunt Horry. But," looking at her with a mixture of cynicism and something unusually watchful in his expression, "I feel sure you'll appreciate my anxiety to have a little protection during her visit, and what better protection could a man have from a former fiancée than another fiancée? That's why I say you can't run out on me!"

Karen sat absolutely still and studied him attentively for several seconds. She was not sure how she felt about this request of his that she should act a part already distasteful to her for some while longer, under circumstances which might make it much more than distasteful, but she did know that she was secretly rather amazed within herself because of the feeling of indignation which had risen up in her when he had let her into the secret of what had happened to him not much more than two years ago.

He who had been so kind to her—who had placed her within the sanctuary of his own house, and surrounded her with every comfort, done everything he could to restore her to health—was not the sort of man to be treated in such a cruel fashion by a woman! She felt so indignant that she actually quivered a little with it, and it showed in her eyes, and her tightening lips. She felt she despised the woman, and could do nothing but loathe her.

No wonder that in spite of their enforced intimacy, all the long evenings, and the many daylight hours, they had spent together, there had always been that something about him which had baffled her. He was impervious—safely entrenched behind the armor of what had probably been the one great love of his life—to any other woman, whether young or old, beautiful or just a rather colorless slip of a girl like herself, who had fainted in his arms on a railway station platform! It wasn't that she had ever wanted him to pay her any serious attention—even to notice her, apart from the ridiculous helplessness which had claimed his sympathy—but even if she had, he would *not* have noticed her! In spite of their pretended engagement, which surely didn't deceive even the servants, she might have been a member of his own sex who was enjoying his hospitality, and benefiting from his undoubted kindness. A young boy in his house, someone who aroused a certain protective instinct in him, but who would never get behind the uniformative mask of his face and really know him.

And he had been hurt by a woman who was now proposing to step back into his life and perhaps hurt him again! It was preposterous—it was unthinkable! Her quivering indignation told her that something must be done about it.

"How long is she likely to stay?" she asked. "This —this ex-fiancée of yours?"

"I haven't any idea," he replied, with a return of his usual lazy smile, "but I wouldn't demand your protection too long if you felt the situation was impossible."

She was silent again for perhaps another full minute, and then she said quietly:

"I don't suppose it would be all that impossible, as I've already posed as your fiancée for nearly a month. And I feel that I owe you something. It's been worrying me that I couldn't think of a way in which I could repay you for all that you've done for me. But if — if deceiving your aunt, and this — this Fiona — would be some sort of repayment, then I'm quite willing to continue with the deception."

For a moment she was surprised because he did not appear to grasp at her ready compliance with all the gratification she had expected of him, and in fact, just for a bare half-second, she thought that something in his face was an indication that he was uncertain. He looked at her, and the cool grey eyes seemed to soften in a way they had never quite done before, and she felt that he was about to say something almost impetuous.

But if he was he changed his mind, and instead he said, with just the merest touch of mockery in his smile:

"Well, in that case, I shall probably have cause to be grateful to you—and I am grateful to you now! But I don't really think I shall seriously require any protection from Mrs. Barrington. It would be flattering myself too much if I imagined that she still had any interest in me, but she was always very fond of my aunt. However, on the principle that there are as good fish in the sea as ever came out of it, the fact that you are apparently willing to consider me as a life partner will remove any impression that I've become a woman-hater, or something of the sort, all as the result of one ill-fated romance."

"There's just one thing," Karen said diffidently, as she stared at the fire in order to avoid having to meet his eyes. "You don't think that perhaps—that when you see her again you might wish—wish you hadn't attempted to deceive her? Discover that you don't need any protection——?"

He shook his head, his expression bleak again.

"Even allowing for the fact that the flesh is weak, I don't think so," he answered.

But Karen wondered, as she ventured to steal another look at his face.

He glanced up quickly and met her eyes, smiling a little mockingly as he asked:

"Well? What is it you want to know?"

"Is she attractive?" Karen asked.

"Fiona Barrington?" He lay back in his chair and studied the glowing logs in the fire. "She was much more than attractive and she can't have altered greatly in less than three years. She is also extremely beautiful, and although beauty is in the eye of the beholder, I think most people would agree with me that she is—quite something!"

"I see," Karen said, and her voice sounded rather flat.

CHAPTER SIX

THE NEXT DAY SHE had a letter from Nannie McBain, full of affection and concern for her welfare, and stating plainly that there was little likelihood of her being back at her cottage for several weeks to come. But the letter concluded on a relieve note, because she had heard all about Karen's engagement to Iain

Mackenzie, and although Ellen was obviously puzzled as to how this had come about, she was also delighted. The Mackenzies were a fine family, and Craigie House was so near to her own cottage that it would be lovely when she did finally return home to know that in future she would be living practically on Karen's own doorstep. Karen was a lucky girl, and she congratulated her very heartily.

Karen felt slightly appalled when she had got to the end of this letter, pleased though she was to have at last some direct contact with her old nurse, and she carried it down into the library where the master of the place was at that moment sorting his own letters, and showed it to him.

After he had read it he looked up at her with an unmistakably amused grin.

"Amazing, isn't it, the way news gets around? And to think we've been snowed up for the past month."

Karen's blue eyes looked dark with apprehension as she gazed at him.

"Are you quite sure we're not storing up for ourselves a lot of trouble?"

"My dear child, what trouble could you store up for yourself?" he demanded lightly, as he carelessly ripped up a pile of envelopes and dropped them into the wastepaper basket. "When the time comes you've merely got to let it be known that you couldn't endure the thought of marrying me after all, and just drift away out of my life! It will be simplicity itself, and in the meantime I'm helping you to solve your own most urgent problem."

He glanced out of the window at the sun, making a splendor of the lawn that had been so recently hidden beneath a mantle of snow, and he added as if he had received a sudden inspiration

"And do you know what I'm going to do now? I'm going to get out the car and take you for a short drive, which will at least be a change for you. So pop upstairs to your room and wrap yourself up warmly. We mustn't risk your catching a chill, but we must let you have a little air."

The drive was such a successful experiment that it was repeated the following day, and although on the first day they merely drove through the village and then back home by a road which brought them to the rear of Craigie House, the second day they ventured farther afield. It was so beautifully warm on this day that spring itself might have been just around the corner, and Karen's eyes were gladdened by the prospect of brown fields lying open now to the kiss of the sun, and scarlet berries in the hedgerows that told their tale of a hard winter drawing rapidly nearer to its close. There was even a faint touch of scarlet in her own cheeks when she got out of the car at the completion of that day's drive, and although she was certain that heads had popped out of doorways, and faces had watched them behind curtains, as the big black Mackenzie car stole silently through the village and between the rows of cottages, she had thoroughly enjoyed it.

Iain looked at her approvingly.

"Tomorrow," he said, "we'll try a short walk, and test the strength of those legs of yours."

The walk, too, was something which Karen remembered in after days as having a strange quality of magic about it, for apart from discovering that her legs were perfectly well able to support the rest of her slender body as she started on her first real bit of exercise for weeks, the path they took and the hidden corners of the grounds they visited convinced her, if she had needed any convincing, that Craigie House, in its setting of woods and distant mountains, was far more beautiful than anything she had ever known at such close quarters.

In not much more than a few weeks the gardens would be a blaze of every sort of spring flower, and already they were unfolding themselves timorously in sheltered corners. There would be wave after wave of daffodils sweeping down to the shores of the lake, where the brown reeds bent backwards from the steel-grey water, and the little island in the centre of it, which seemed to be placidly afloat, would be a film of new green leaves instead of a wilderness of bare branches.

Under the sheltered south side of the house there would be wallflowers scenting the air with their sweetness as the spring advanced, and the long grass of the orchard would be starred with white narcissi. Looking even farther ahead, into the long summer days, Karen could imagine the peace that would be like a benediction over Craigie while the hours were filled with sunshine, and the lawns would look like emerald velvet under the clear, cool blue of the northern sky. The evenings would be full of the scents of clove pinks the drawing-room cascading roses from every vase, and the sun went down at last, the mountains, that were still grim and forbidding on a day in February, would look dreamy and remote under the first light of the stars.

She could see it all so clearly that it was almost as if she had the power of second sight, but her heart felt a little heavy when she remembered that in the summer she would not be there. She would be back in London, in her microscopic flat, working for some-one like her old employer, who would demand nothing more of her than that she should receive his dictation and type his letters with a fair amount of a dequacy, and then allow her to go home at night to cook her own supper over a gas ring.

But as she walked the paths of Craigie with Iain Mackenzie at her side, and everywhere the air was full of the sound of water that had started to bubble and not merely to flow free of ice once more, and birdsong that was a little premature because winter might yet have a final fling in reserve, she was con-scious of feeling physically so very much stronger that future events were just then more or less un-important, and when they arrived back at the house her host's chief concern was that he had not over-tired her and that she was warm after her walk.

He looked somewhat doubtfully at her tweed coat, even after she had assured him that she was beautifully warm, and, in fact, glowing after the unaccustomed excercise.

"You don't seem to me to be wrapped up as much as you should be," he remarked. He felt the shoulder of the tweed coat. "Is this really thick enough for a winter coat?"

She knew what he was thinking—that her clothes were none of them up to the standard he would have looked for in a reasonably well-dressed woman, and she felt herself flushing as a sudden thought attacked her.

"You don't think your aunt and Mrs Barrington, when they arrive, will think I'm a little—well, shabby, for your fiancée?" she asked instead of answering his question.

"My dear girl, what a ridiculous question," he answered, looking down into her upraised, sensitive face. "And, in any case, I wasn't thinking of shabbiness."

"No, perhaps you weren't, but Mrs. Barrington isn't in the least shabby, is she?"

He smiled with obvious amusement.

"She used to be very much the reverse, but perhaps widowhood has changed her in some respects."

"I should hardly think so," Karen remarked, as if a good deal of the enjoyment of her walk had already departed from her. "Smart women don't generally become dowdy even as a result of losing their husbands."

Then she went away upstairs to remove the offending coat.

When she came down to dinner that night she was wearing a little cherry-red dress that was the only really expensive purchase she had made since she had started to earn her own living, and at least she was not ashamed of it. The color did something to emphasize the extreme delicacy of her appearance, and her host stared at her rather hard when they sat facing one another at the table.

For the first time since he had brought her to Craigie he was wearing a dinner-jacket, and she thought how well it became him, and how undeniably attractive he was in the soft light of the candles. They flickered in tall, Georgian candlesticks, and the rest of the table was heavily loaded with Georgian silver, although there were only the two of them.

Iain looked along it and said suddenly and almost abruptly to the girl at the opposite end:

"There's something I want to ask you, Karen. Will you become engaged to me in earnest?"

Karen set down the small silver spoon with which she had been coping with her sweet and looked at him in astonishment.

"Whatever for?" she asked

Prout, the parlormaid, returned with their coffee, and when she had pored it out she brought bottles of liqueur from the sideboard and set them on the table Karen shook her head when Iain offered her a brilliantly green chartreuse, and as soon as the maid had departed again she said with an odd, uncertain note in her voice,

"Are you really asking me to marry you?"

"I am." He was frowning at the bottles and not looking at her. "I think if you would consider it, it would solve quite a few of your problems, and there are other reasons why I personally feel it would be a good idea."

"What other reasons?"

He looked at her this time, and his look was contemplative—probing.

"Oh, there are quite a few of them, really, but the main one is that you need looking after. I'm a little bit concerned about you because I don't quite know what you are going to do when you leave here, and I feel very strongly that you ought not to be allowed to leave at all. Also—well, Craigie can do with a mistress, someone to run the place. And I'm sure you could do that quite adequately."

Karen stared at the green chartreuse he had poured out for himself, and she hoped he was not aware of the fact that a pulse at the base of her throat was beating like a frightened bird imprisioned in a cage, and that she was feeling a little sick inside at the same time. It was the coat, she told herself dully. The coat had caused him to make up his mind about this, and in order that she should be provided with suitable coats, and alarm no more strangers by fainting in their arms at inopportune moments, he was prepared to marry her. He was also a little afraid because Fiona Barrington was coming back into his life, and he had no desire to fall a victim to her a second time. He was probably well aware that there was a very grave danger of his doing so, but if only he really was engaged to be married—or, better still, actually married!—then the danger could not touch him. He was playing for safety, and he thought she did not know it!

"Well?" he asked, as she made no attempt to answer him.

She lifted grave, but otherwise slightly inscrutable, blue eyes from the liquid in his glass, and gazed at him.

"No," she answered, shaking her head, "no, I couldn't marry you."

His eyes lifted slightly.

"You're quite sure about that?"

"Quite sure."

"Very well," he murmured, the tone of his voice providing her with no clue to what he was thinking. "We won't discuss the matter again, but it struck me this afternoon that it was a good idea, that's all!"

Then he rose and pushed back his chair, and as she walked ahead of him into the drawing-room he suggested that they should play chess.

"Or shall we try something else for a change?" he further suggested. "What about two-handed rummy, or picquet? Can you play picquet?"

He brought out the cards, and set the little table up between them, and as he proceeded to instruct her the art of a card game she had not so far attempted to play she found herself watching him and feeling curiously fascinated by the sight of his bent head and absorbed expression. He might have asked her in the dining-room just now to let him run her in to the nearest town to do some shopping, or something of the sort, and not anything as momentous as whether or not she could bring herself to marry him.

Marry him! . . .

Somehow she was not even quite certain that she had heard him aright. If it had been a serious proposal it had been so casually made that surely no other woman had ever received one quite like it before! . . . "Craigie can do with a mistress, someone to run the place. And I'm sure you could do that quite adequately." She took a deep breath, and wondered how she would be feeling at this moment if she had said "Yes."

She stared hard at his hands—such beautifully shaped hands, strong and capable, with admirably cared-for finger nails, that were dealing expertly with the cards. There was a gold signet ring on one of his little fingers, and it winked like a bright eye in the fireglow. The white line of his cuff as it escaped from the blackness of his sleeve was almost startingly immaculate, and an equally white handkerchief tucked partly up his sleeve brushed the top of the table as he demonstrated with the pack.

Karen lifted her eyes to his face, and not for the first time she thought what an utterly purposeful line of jaw he had. There was no weakness about the mouth, either; it was an attractive mouth when he smiled in a certain fashion, because there was something faintly provocative about his smile. His eyes reminded her of the grey of roof slates with the frost upon them when he was not smiling, but at other times they could resemble the grey running of the stream at the bottom of the garden, quiet but buoyant, deceptively placid, sparkling in the sunlight. And the sleek smoothness of his hair, so dark that it made her think of a blackbird's plumage.

If only she had said "Yes" she could spend the rest of her life like this, watching him whenever she wanted to do so, knowing that he would never be far away, that he was someone who had taken upon himself the right to care for her and look after her. Craigie would be her home, and the seasons would come and go there, and everything would be very peaceful, because Craigie was peaceful. . . . But, above all, if she had said "Yes" she would have the right to call herself the wife of Iain Mackenzie! . . .

She felt that excitable little pulse beating wildly again in her throat, and for a solitary instant she wondered just as wildly as the pulse was beating why she had not said "Yes." And then as he looked up and met her eyes she felt the vivid pink dye her cheeks, and she looked away abashed—terrified lest he should be able to read in her face the thoughts she had been thinking.

But all he said was:

"Are you a little bit tired tonight? Would you rather go to bed and learn this game another night? We mustn't forget you've had rather a lot of fresh air today—for you—and you're probably sleepy."

She agreed at once that she was, and as he stood up to open the door for her she felt anxious to dart past him wildly and escape. But instead she forced herself to walk sedately towards the foot of the stairs, and although she knew he was still watching her she mounted them slowly.

But she thought in almost a frantic fashion: "He must have guessed! . . . I'm *sure* he guessed! . . ."

CHAPTER SEVEN

TWO DAYS LATER Aunt Horatia Montagu-Jackson and Mrs. Barrington arrived just in time for lunch, without any warning whatsoever. They drove up in an old-fashioned chauffeur-driven Daimler. Aunt Horry was wearing tweeds and a hat rather like a Tyrolean hat, with a feather stuck in it. She was small but agile, with grey hair and a pair of bright blue eyes that beamed from under the Tyrolean hat, and an incongruous note was added to her appearance by a great many diamonds, in the shape of brooches, braclets and ear-rings, that adorned her diminutive person.

She advanced upon her nephew when he arrived to greet her in the hall and embraced him with obvious fervor, kissing him heartily on both cheeks.

"You look," she told him, "extraordinarily well, and I'm delighted to see you."

"And you," he told her, "don't look even half a day older!"

"My dear, I'm being treated by a wonderful Italian doctor who's performed miracles—simply miracles! —for my rheumatism, and in fact I just haven't got it any more!" She looked around her as if searching for someone, and then exclaimed quickly: "But where's the young woman? My new niece-to-be! I must see her—I must see her at once, because I've been simply dying to know what she looks like!"

As Karen emerged from the shadows of the hall she felt rather than saw the keen blue eyes fasten upon her, and then Aunt Horatio darted forward and caught her by her slender shoulders and looked at he so hard that the girl's blush rose uncontrolably.

"H'm!" the elderly lady exclaimed, at the end of her inspection, and then "h'm!" again. She sent an oddly quizzical sideways glance at her nephew, lighty patted Karen's cheek, and then released her. And then they all turned as footsteps sounded at the end of the hall near the open front door, and Fiona Barrington appeared, moving gracefully towards them, with her arms full of flowers and parcels she had stopped to collect from inside the car. It was a habit of Mrs. Montagu-Jackson's—her husband had been Montagu Jackson, who made a fortune out of baby powder and other nursery toilet requisites many years before he died, and after his death she had decided to give herself a double-barrelled name by including his Christian name—to bring with her, on her visits to her nephew, large quantities of useful provender, such as eggs from her own farm, and vegetables cultivated by her gardener, being firmly of the opinion that they were always most acceptable to a bachelor. So behind Mrs. Barrington came the chauffeur who maintained the Daimler at such a shining pitch of perfection, bearing the heavier articles which the slight figure of the widow could hardly be expected to carry.

Karen, who realized that she had been waiting with something not nearly so stimulating as curiosity for this moment, knew that all her worst fears were instantly realized when she took her first look at Fiona Barrington.

To begin with, the coat she was wearing was so obviously mink that Karen's heart dropped like a plummet when she remembered her own cheap tweed. And she was wearing a little mink cap, too, specially designed to call attention to corn-silk hair. Not *fair* hair, like Karen's own, but a deep, shining, lustrous gold.

Her eyes were golden, too—golden as quartz or topaz—and they were smiling in an enchanting way under the mink cap. She couldn't have been much older than Karen herself, in spite of her widowhood, but she had all the sophistication and the poise in the world, and as she shook hands with Karen the latter caught the first faint breath of the delicate perfume she brought with her, like something belonging exclusively to Paris in the springtime.

"And this is the little fiancée?" she said, and just as Aunt Horatio had done she shot a sudden, sideways glance at Iain's face that had the merest suspicion of something both quizzical and amused in it.

Mackenzie's face remained cool and slightly aloof —an expression that had appeared in it the instant he had ceased greeting his aunt. But Karen did not dare to look at him, and she only knew that she herself had failed to create an impression that could quite truthfully be described as favorable—or, at any rate, she had been something of a surprise to both of these women visitors. Although she was wearing her best tweed skirt, and a jumper that was neat and unspectacular, she had all the colorlessness of an invalid about her—or one who was only just ceasing to be an invalid — and it was plain at a glance that she lacked both confidence and poise, and moreover that she was almost desperately shy and aware of how badly she fitted in just then.

She wanted to escape with Mrs. Burns when the housekeeper appeared to receive instructions about extra places at the luncheon table; and she would have been happy to have been simply Prout, whose only task was to hand round drinks in the drawing-room before they all went in to the meal. But she was the prospective mistress of the house, or so they all fondly believed, and she could not merely sit tongue-tied and afraid that if she did open her lips she might say something unwise and foolish that would glaringly proclaim her to be acting a part.

It was not so bad while lunch was in progress, for the service of the meal caused enough diversion, and Mrs. Burns was agitated because she had not known beforehand that the visitors were preparing to descend upon them. She infected Prout with some of her own agitation as a result of supervising her too closely whenever they were in the dining-room together, until, in order to pour oil on the troubled waters, Aunt Horatia declared when they were nearing the coffee stage that the lunch was far more perfect than anything she ever enjoyed in her own house, and Mrs. Burns at least was happy again.

Iain, too, while they will still seated at the long table in the dining-room, was careful to give Karen all the support he could, and dangerous topics like how long he and Karen had been engaged to be married, exactly where they met, and when they were proposing to get married, were skilfully side-tracked by him in favor of his aunt's rheumatism, and the wonderful cure for which the Italian doctor was responsible.

But once back in the drawing-room after lunch, Karen knew that the real attack was coming. Mrs. Montagu-Jackson managed to install herself in a chair close to Karen's, while Mrs. Barrington occupied a corner of a Chesterfield and successfully persuaded her host to desert his post in the middle of the rug before the fireplace and talk to her about his recent travels abroad.

Out of the corner of her eye Karen could see that he gravitated somewhat unwillingly to the side of the lovely widow—for anyone more deserving of the appellation "lovely" Karen had never seen — and Mrs. Barrington produced a long turquoise holder from her handbag and allowed him to light the cigarette she placed in it. Then Aunt Horatia began to talk to Karen in a friendly, sociable manner, and her opening gambit was very much to the point.

"And now, my dear," she said, as if she was going to suggest getting to know one another, "you can tell me the truth about yourself and Iain!"

Karen looked at her, faintly horrified, but Aunt Horatia was lying back in her chair and smiling comfortably.

"Go on, you silly child, and don't be afraid of me! I'm not easily shocked, I can assure you."

And so, in view of the fact that it was plainly not much use dissembling, Karen told her the truth—all the truth that is, apart from the actual falsity of her engagement, which, because she had given her promise to Iain, she did not disclose to his aunt. And at the end of her simple recital Mrs. Montagu-Jackson nodded her head, as if it was all much as she had expected, and observed:

"Well, that's all quite understandable but it was quixotic of you both to become engaged—at least, it was quixotic of Iain, but I haven't quite made up my mind about you yet."

Karen felt a tiny, cold feeling stealing about her heart, as if something she had been hugging to herself recently as precious was likely to be snatched away from her altogether. She looked at the elder lady with vaguely troubled eyes.

"You—you haven't made up your mind about—me?"

"No, my dear." The old eyes were gentle, and the voice had a sympathetic note in it. "You appear to have had quite a lot to put up with in the way of illness, and I'd say at this moment you are far from strong, and Iain can be terribly kind when he feels like it—I know that! But you can't marry a man because he'd kind, or because he offers you a home."

"N-no," Karen agreed, and wished that this visitation from Iain's relative had been postponed until she was feeling just a little stronger than she was at present, and therefore more capable of putting up some sort of camouflage.

"On the other hand, if you're really sure——" There was a pause, and Aunt Horatia glanced for a moment at her nephew's face as he sat beside his glamorous ex-fiancée on the Chesterfield—"you could do much, much worse for yourself!"

Karen said nothing, and Aunt Horry dived into her handbag for her cigarette-case, from which she extracted a fat and faintly greyish-looking cigarette.

"I have these made specially for me," she explained, "and they'd be much too strong for a young girl like you—a mixture of Egyptian and Turkish tobaccos—so I'm not going to offer you one."

She surrounded herself with a blue haze of smoke which smelled strongly of the interior of some exotic eastern quarter, and at the same time she thoughtfully studied Karen.

"I'm going to make a suggestion," she said. "I've explained that I'm not easily shocked, and neither am I, but I don't think it's quite right for a young thing like you to be living here alone with a bachelor of nearly thirty-five, even though you *are* thinking of getting married!" Her glance at the girl stated plainly that she doubted that, and she continued: "In my house you can be a guest for as long as you like, and no one can say a thing about you—and Iain can come and see you as often as he wants to! So I suggest you pack up your things, or get Mrs. Burns to pack them up for you, and come back with Fiona and me this afternoon!"

At first Karen was not quite certain that the older woman was entirely serious, but when she realized that she was, and, moreover, that in spite of the kindliness and the gentleness in her expression there was some extra quality which would be difficult to combat if, and when, her mind was made up about something, feeling of almost profound dismay descended upon her. She felt exactly as if the suggestion had been made that she desert a proven and safe harbor for all the unknown dangers of the high seas, and she stammered:

"Go-go back with you?"

"Yes, my dear, I think it's a splendid idea!" Having given birth to the idea Mrs. Montagu-Jackson beamed at her again. "I've a young man coming to stay with me next week — my godson, Aubrey Ainsworth, who is beginning to make a name for himself as one of these futuristic painters, or whatever they call themselves—and with Fiona, who has promised to stay with me more or less indefinitely, we shall be quite a jolly party. I simply love having people to stay with me, and what you badly need, my child, is a change. You've been cooped up here long enough, and however devoted you are to Iain it will be good for both of you to have a breather from one another for a short while at least."

She looked across at her nephew and instantly claimed his attention by announcing that she had formed what she was convinced was an excellent plan. When he had heard what the plan was he, like Karen, looked a little taken aback. Then one of his dark eyebrows ascended half humorously.

"Is that really necessary?" he asked. "I mean, don't you think Mrs. Burns—to say nothing of Annie, and Prout, and George, who also live in the house—can provide adequate chaperonage for Karen? Or are you afraid she's being neglected? I can assure you she's looking very, very much better now than she did when she first came here——"

"My dear boy, none of that enters into it," his aunt assured him, waving the remains of her specially blended cigarette in the air. "I'm not old-fashioned, as you know, and I'd trust Mrs. Burns to look after even the most guileless young creature who entered your house. But Karen's had a bout of illness and been confined to one place for far too long, with no companionship save your own, and I feel that if she's going to get really well and strong again something will have to be done about it. I can look after her just as well as you can, you know, and Fiona can lend a hand. In fact, we shall just love having her."

"Of course we will," Fiona put in swiftly, in a soft and slightly husky voice, which Karen had already decided was one of the most attractive things about her. Another attractive thing was the way her golden eyes melted whenever she was just about to break into a smile, and the almost tender curve of her full scarlet lips when the smile touched them was something, almost, to watch for. It made of the smile a thing of indescribable charm, with the power to bestow something in the nature of a caress. "It will be really nice."

Iain turned to her, an ironical gleam in his eyes. "*You* think so?" he asked.

"I do," she assured him. "And I agree with your aunt that it is a little dull here for Karen at the present stage of her convalescence, but unlike your aunt I *am* a little bit old-fashioned, and I do feel that in Karen's best interests, even if you're proposing to get married very soon, it will be as well if she doesn't remain here under your roof more or less indefinitely—until you get married, that is!"

He regarded her with an odd curve to his lips.

"And the fact that she has already been here a month shocks you rather badly, does it?" he enquired in the driest of tones.

"Not at all, darling," she answered soothingly—she even placed one of her white hands lightly, caressingly, on his arm—"but it has probably shocked Mrs. Burns, if one were in a position to find out the truth! And now that you're no longer cut off by weather condition, and we are only too willing to carry Karen away with us, I don't really think you ought to oppose your aunt's suggestion."

"I haven't said I'm going to oppose it," he answered, a little shortly. "But it's rather limited notice, and I don't know that Karen ought to go out again today. It's not as fine as it was yesterday——"

"*Darling,*" Fiona laughed softly, beside him, "a journey of three or four miles, and no more, in a closed and *heated* car? Isn't your concern a little excessive, and aren't you afraid that you won't see as much of her as you have done? Which simply means that we shall expect you to visit us very often, and that will be nice for all of us."

"*Very* nice," Aunt Horatia agreed.

He looked across at Karen with an expression she had never seen on his face before. She felt that behind it lay a feeling of annoyance, mixed with the conviction that he was temporarily cornered, and that he also saw something humorous in the cornering.

"Well, what has Karen got to say" he asked. "Are you growing very bored with my undiluted society, Karen? And do you feel that your reputation will be saved if you leave Craigie for the time being?"

Karen knew very well what she wanted to say, but she was very much afraid of saying it — not only because of his aunt and his ex-fiancée, but because of him, too. If she looked across at him in an openly pleading fashion, and said that she didn't want to leave him, what kind of construction would he place on such a confession as that?

"I—I——" she was beginning, when Aunt Horry came to her rescue.

"Don't be silly, Iain," she said. "Naturally Karen wouldn't tell you if she was bored with you, and as she knows she's coming back here before very long as mistress of the place she's not likely to break her heart because of a few weeks' absence. And that reminds me—*have* you made any plans yet about the wedding? Because if you haven't I'm quite sure the most sensible idea would be to let Karen be married from my house. It's so long since anyone got married from Auchenwiel that it will do the place good, and there's nothing that really appeals to me more than all the fuss and preparation for a wedding."

Iain continued to smile faintly as his eyes met Karen's but the eyes themselves were inscrutable, and he made a shrugging movement with his shoulders.

"I can see that whatever my opinion happens to be on this question of moving Karen it isn't very important," he observed, "but you needn't start wedding preparations yet, Aunt, because Karen and I haven't even fixed a date for taking one another for better or worse. And I hope that you'll leave us to make that decision ourselves, at least."

He stood up and wandered to the window, looking out at the greyness of the afternoon.

"Don't think I'm inhospitable," he said, "but if you're going to taken Karen you'd better leave fairly soon, otherwise you'll be in for some more bad weather. I'll ring for Mrs. Burns," and he pressed the bell for his housekeeper with a somewhat grim expression clinging about his mouth.

Karen did not dare to look at him again. She went meekly up to her room and helped Mrs. Burns with her simple packing, and when it was finished the housekeeper looked at her with a faintly regretful expression in her eyes.

"I'll be glad to see you back again, Miss," she stated with obvious truthfulness, "only when you come back again you'll be Madam, won't you?" She smiled hearteningly. "You'll like Mrs. Montagu-Jackson. She talks a lot, and she's a bit obstinate, but she thinks the world of Mr. Iain, and she must like you, too, or she wouldn't have asked you to stay with her. And perhaps after all she's wise," she added, in a kind of reflective way which, however, passed Karen by altogether, for she was feeling too strangely miserable inside at the thought of leaving the quiet sanctuary of this room which for five weeks now had been hers.

CHAPTER EIGHT

AUCHENWIEL, WHEN THEY arrived there, was a surprise to Karen, for it was completely unlike Craigie House. To begin with it was very large and very pretentious, and with its pepper-box towers and high walls looked like a copy of an old French chateau. Which, in point of fact, was exactly what it was, for the late Montagu Jackson, after a visit with his wife to the South of France, had had it built on the site of a really old building which he had ruthlessly pulled down, and in the full broad light of day, with the Scottish mountains rising behind it, moorland on two sides of it, and a deep glen on the other, it looked a little astonishing.

But when Karen arrived it was very nearly dark, and the thing that impressed her most about it was its size, and the blaze of light that seemed to be pouring from every window.

Inside, she was met with an almost overpowering warmth from central heating, vast areas of rich, thick, crimson carpet, suits of armor that looked a little incongruous standing at the bottom of a fan-shaped staircase, and many massive portraits hanging on panelled walls. Her room, when she reached it, had the impersonal luxury of a hotel bedroom—that is to say, of a five-star hotel. There was a telephone beside the bed, a suite of walnut furniture, a superbly comfortably adjustable chair with a foot-rest, and a little table loaded with magazines beside it; and the enormous built-in cupboards were so capacious that her entire wardrobe, once it had been unpacked, was completely lost in them.

Aunt Horry accompanied her upstairs to her room, and bustled about making sure everything was as she had ordered it to be over the telephone before leaving Craigie House. Then when she looked at Karen she saw that the girl was utterly devoid of color, and plainly almost exhausted after her ascent of the great, sweeping staircase. She ordered her into bed at once.

"And you can have your dinner brought to you on a tray," she said. She lightly pinched Karen's cheek. "I want you to be happy here, and although you're bound to feel strange for a day or two, you'll very soon get used to us, and Iain isn't very far away, you know. He'll be coming over to see us quite often, I expect."

Then with a smile which was meant to be encouraging she departed from the room, leaving Karen feeling as if she was spiritually as well as physically limp. Moreover, she felt bereft — bereft and forlorn, and as alone as she had felt when she first came out of hospital, which was absurd when she was surrounded by nothing but luxury and the excellent intentions of a hostess who loved entertaining visitors.

She was just about to remove her clothes and climb into the truly marvellous-looking bed, with its fine fat pillows and its hem-stitched sheets, when a maid knocked on her door and announced that she had instructions to run her a bath, and that she was also bringing her dinner up to her later on. The girl was smart and friendly—not, however, dear and familiar like Prout, or Annie, or Mrs. Burns—and she looked at Karen sympathetically before she went on her way to the white-tiled bathroom.

Just before a hollow booming noise, which Karen recognized was a dinner-gong, rose up from the hall, there came another light tap on her door, and in response to her "Come in" Fiona Barrington entered.

She changed in to a dinner-gown of superb tawny-gold velvet, and she looked like a golden girl, especially as there was a curious snaky gold necklace about her slender throat, and on her arms gold bracelets which were inset with stones like garnets.

She was smiling as she came into the room, and she perched herself on the foot of the bed and looked at Karen.

"Quite comfortable?" she asked. "I must say you certainly look it, but you also look a little bit lost in that bed. There isn't very much of you, is there?"

"I'm a bit thin at the moment," Karen admitted, feeling awkward as she set down her soup-spoon and wished that this glamorous vision had not appeared just as she was trying to work up an appetite for her dinner, served to her on a daintily-laid tray. "But that's usual after two doses of fairly severe illness. And I'm already putting on weight—I'll be quite plump again in a few weeks."

"Will you?" But there was a faintly amused, faintly sceptical look in the topaz eyes. "To me that's a little difficult to imagine. I'd describe you as a kind of windflower of a girl, never likely to be really substantial, and always in danger of being blown away altogether. I imagine Iain rather shares my views, and that's why he's so terribly concerned about you, and didn't want to run any risks this afternoon."

"Oh"—Karen felt herself flushing—"as to that, I've already given quite a lot of trouble to Mrs. Burns and Annie, and it would be too bad if I had to occupy much of their time again."

"And you imagine that sort of consideration weighs with Iain?" Fiona looked even more amused.

Karen deliberately avoided her eyes.

"I think it would," she answered quietly, "because he does study the people around him, and in any case he knows I'd hate to give any more trouble than I have already given."

Mrs. Barrington's softly brilliant smile became more gentle.

"You're quite sweet, you know," she said, and put out a hand and lightly touched Karen's. "In fact, I think you're very sweet! And you've also had rather a bad time lately!"

"It—it wasn't too bad," Karen stammered.

"But all the same, it's high time you had a change—that's why I'm glad we brought you here. And if you're wise, and it's fine tomorrow, you'll come with me on a trip into Inverlochie. I want to do some shopping, but you can just sit in the car and take things easily, unless you'd like to do a little shopping also?" Her eyes went to the simple pink nightdress the girl in the bed was wearing, which, although it was hand-embroidered by Karen herself, who was a skilled needlewoman, was not the kind of nightdress the lovely widow would be likely to wear. "There must be a few things you're needing, and shops are always stimulating. And we can have coffee at the George. What do you say?"

"I think it would be very nice," Karen replied uncertainly, and Mrs. Barrington slipped from the bed.

"Very well then! That's agreed—provided, of course, its fine! And now I really must go, because the gong's already sounded, and I'm several minutes late."

But she moved unhurriedly towards the door, smiling at Karen until it had closed behind her, and then the girl in the bed looked down thoughtfully again at her soup, but made no attempt to drink any more of it.

Later that night she lay in her bed and stared at the firelight flickering on the ceiling, and the flood of golden light cast by the golden-shaded bedside lamp on the apple green carpet. This room had just as much comfort as her room at Craigie House, perhaps even more, but she felt utterly alone and comfortless in it, and as she turned her face into her pillow she felt inclined to weep—weep for all that she had left behind, all that was no longer part of her daily life, that she might never see again!

And then all at once the telephone on the bedside table beside her shrilled, and her heart gave a great uneasy bound as she looked at it on its ivory rest. She put out a tentative hand and picked up the receiver, and the next moment she was ready to cry with relief because the voice which came to her over the wire was so exquisitely familiar.

"Hullo," it said, "is that you, Karen! Iain here."

Iain here! . . .

She swallowed twice, to rid her throat of the lump in it, and forced her pulses to cease behaving like wild creatures imprisoned in a zoo, and managed to say almost steadily:

"Oh, how nice! How nice of you to bother about me! Unless there's something—something you want to tell me? . . ."

She heard him laugh softly, as if amused.

"What would I be likely to want to tell you at this hour of the night?" She heard him wait for her answer, and when it did not come he continued, as if still amused: "No, my dear, I was quite well aware you'd have a telephone beside your bed—Auchenwiel has every luxury! — and I thought it just as likely that you might still be awake, and perhaps feeling rather strange. So I decided a familiar voice would probably do you good."

"Oh!" Karen exclaimed, and he could hear her breath catch. "I was—and it has!"

"Good!" he answered, softly. "Then it's a good thing I remembered how well you were equipped, isn't it?"

"Yes."

"But you're not really hating things, are you?"

"No"—a little uncertainly — "no; I'm not hating things."

"I'll admit it was all a bit of a rush, your departure, but Aunt Horry really will look after you, you know, and perhaps a bachelor establishment was not the best place for you just now. But I'll be seeing you fairly often, and as a matter of fact I've received an invitation for this coming week-end. Do you think you could endure to have me about you again so soon?"

Karen refrained from answering him immediately, because she knew that if she obeyed every impulse in her body she would simply cry out to him over the dividing telephone wire that already she was missing him so badly that it was a kind of private agony. She had been wondering how she was going to endure it for long if she was not to see him again soon.

"Well?" he asked, as he did not answer him, and his voice was a little sharp.

"Of course I'll be very happy to see you again," she managed then, and she felt she could almost see him smiling at the other end of the line.

"That's splendid!" he exclaimed. "And now," he added, "go to sleep. You really ought to have been asleep about an hour ago."

"I'm not very tired," she breathed back.

"No, but go to sleep."

"I will," she promised.

"Good night, my dear."

"Good night."

"I've got a name, you know," he reminded her.

"Good night, Iain."

"Sleep well, little one," he answered her.

And she quietly laid the telephone back on its rest and slid down into her bed and gripped hard at the frilly edge of her pillow-case. As she lay there with closed eyes she was recapturing every single moment of that telephone conversation, and every vibration in the voice that had spoken to her. She felt now that he had spoken to her she might be able to sleep—she was even happy to go to sleep, because in her dreams she might be back with him again at Craigie House.

CHAPTER NINE

BEFORE THE WEEK-END Aubrey Ainsworth arrived at Auchenwiel, and although she had been rather dreading meeting yet another stranger Karen found him quite a pleasant young man, with none of the usual hallmarks of an artist devoted to modern art. He was about a couple of years older than herself, and had fairish hair rather like her own, grey eyes that were utterly unlike Iain Mackenzie's, and a thin, slightly careworn face.

The carewornness was explained by the fact that he had apparently little money, although his ambition was unbounded. He hoped one day to be as well known as Picasso, and in the meantime he thought he would like to attempt a study of Karen's face and head if she could spare the time to give him a sitting. He told her that there was something in her face which interested him, and that her bone structure was well-nigh perfect. She had a curiously perfect skin, too, although she was so pale, and the tiny blue veins at her temples, and the delicate mauve shadows under her eyes, threw into prominence the perfection of her skin.

"I should imagine you'd tan well," he told her, after a particularly prolonged scrutiny, "but at the moment you look positively ethereal."

Karen smiled, because even though she still looked ethereal she was feeling very much better, and she was sure that was largely due to the fact that she had been out of doors quite a lot since coming to Auchenwiel. The weather had been very kind—it really did look as if spring was on its way—and for that part of the world almost balmy, and although she had not enjoyed the trip to Inverlochie with Mrs. Barrington—for no really good reason that she could explain even to herself, since Mrs. Barrington had been particularly kind and considerate—there was no doubt that such an outing had provided her with a break in the routine of an invalid. They had had coffee at the George, and she had felt that she was once more caught up in the daily life of ordinary human beings. She had bought herself a twin-set which she had known she couldn't really afford, but she had been unable to resist the soft, misty blue of it, which Fiona had insisted was exactly right with her eyes.

She had also, because she felt so dowdy and colorless, bought herself a new lipstick, and some new face-powder which had just the right touch of creaminess in it to deal with her pallor. When she put it on she knew that her skin looked even more perfect—more healthy was the way she put it herself—and the lipstick had a positively magical effect on her lips. They glowed like the pink petals of a flower, and at the same time they were alive and warm and generous.

Aubrey Ainsworth seemed to find it impossible to take his eyes off her when she appeared for the first time wearing her new make-up, and Aunt Horry looked faintly surprised.

"It's extraordinary how illness can pull one down," she said, "and how something fresh in the cosmetic line can do so much for one." She put her head on one side and studied the girl consideringly. When she had first seen her and she had thought her almost painfully plain, and she had been amazed because Iain had announced that he intended to marry her. But now—now she was no longer so certain. The girl had a flower-like beauty which might well pull at the heartstrings of a man like her nephew, who had seen so much of indisputable feminine beauty, and was possibly a little bored by it. The girl, even without her new make-up, had a pathetic poignant quality in her face, and with it she was almost if not quite lovely.

In Iain's eyes she might even be *very* lovely—that intense darkness of his was probably attracted by the extreme fairness of Karen—and if only she were really well dressed she might be capable of dazzling quite a few people.

Aunt Horry began to puzzle her brains as to how she could provide new and suitable clothes for Karen with offending (*a*) the girl herself, and (*b*) her nephew, because it was very likely his intention to provide them for her himself as soon as they were married. But she couldn't be married without a suitable outfit, and something would have to be done about it. She would have to consult Iain, because the girl herself was as poor as a church mouse, although she was very gently bred. In some ways she would not be out of place as the mistress of Craigie House.

On the Saturday afternoon when Iain was due to arrive for his week-end Karen appeared in her new twin-set, and her mirror had told her that it really did suit her. Her eyes were bright and very blue. Inside her she was unable to deny the excitement which coursed through all her veins because the man she was supposed to be engaged to marry was coming to stay at Auchenwiel for at least one night, and perhaps two, and it already felt like years since she had last seen him. There was a faint excited glow in her cheeks, like the blush on a drift of apple blossom, and her lips hardly needed the application of lipstick they received before she went downstairs.

When she heard his car speeding up the drive and then coming to rest at the foot of the flight of steps before the front door her heart started to hammer so wildly that she was afraid those about her would hear it. And then the door was flung open, and Aunt Horry embraced her nephew on her own doorstep, and he kissed her with a light, audacious smile in his eyes. The audacious look was still there when he advanced to greet Karen, and although for a moment surprise at her appearance almost banished it, it was there when he bent to sweep her into a quick embrace also, and she felt his hard masculine mouth claiming hers for a moment.

The color receded from her cheeks, and for one instant she looked so white that she felt everyone looking at her. Then, with a rush, it swept back, over her throat, and chin and brow as well as her soft cheeks, and Iain's eyes were looking into hers with some amusement, although there was also something else very intent in his gaze.

"How delightful you look!" he told her, paying her the normal compliment of a fiancé might be expected to pay under the circumstances, especially when she really did look delightful. "And very much better," he added, more gravely.

"There you are, you see!" Aunt Horry exclaimed triumphantly. "Didn't I tell you I could look after her at this stage of her convalescence better than you could, my dear?"

There was no disputing that she had obviously looked after Karen very well. And then, from the foot of the stairs, Fiona came forward to greet him.

If Karen looked delightful, Mrs. Barrington's appearance was so near perfection that it couldn't fail to bring a glimmer of admiration to any man's eyes. Karen saw it; she noticed that he also seemed to start slightly when Fiona appeared suddenly in front of him, holding out her hand, with his blood-red finger-nails, as if she had taken him aback. She was wearing a fine woollen dress in a burnt amber color, so moulded to the shape of her slender figure that it was almost as revealing as an evening dress. She wore chunky jewellery that appeared to be carved out of jade, and her make-up was exotic. As always she brought her exciting Paris perfume with her.

"Hullo, Iain," she said, and smiled up at him under her entrancing eyelashes. "So you've managed to survive without Karen! And she has just managed to exist without you," stealing a look at the other girl which, although nobody else probably recognized it, contained the merest suspicion of something which could have been a kind of half-affectionate contempt.

"Oh, I don't think I can agree with that," Iain replied, looking more carefully at his fiancée. "Karen has obviously found it very easy to exist without me, which is undoubtedly due to Aunt Horry's skill as a hostess."

But he smiled very gently at Karen nevertheless, and she wanted to assure him that although she was so much better she had been counting the minutes until his coming, and that part of the glow of animation in her face was due to the fact that he had arrived. But this was something she had to keep to herself, as she knew.

She was, however, unreasonably thrilled when he picked up her hand and drew it through his arm, conducting her over to the fireplace in the great library where they were to have tea. And he placed her almost tenderly in one of the comfortable chairs near the blazing logs that were lighting up all the handsome panelling, afterwards taking up his position near her, and giving her a wonderful feeling of being once more under his protection. And although Aubrey Ainsworth waited on her when the tea was brought in on an enormous trolley weighted down with old-fashioned silver and flowery porcelain cups, obviously taking a kind of pleasure in pressing her to an endless assortment of sandwiches and hot cakes, baps and bannocks, Iain merely regarded his efforts with a look of faint amusement, and agreed at once when he somewhat naïvely asked permission to paint her portrait.

"Certainly," he said, "so long as you don't paint her in cubes, or oblongs, or anything of that sort."

And Aubrey looked frankly delighted by the permission obtained, and fell to studying Karen afresh, and with even greater enthusiasm, while he planned the medium he would use for consigning her to canvas.

That night, when they all came down to dinner, Iain was wearing the Highland evening dress in which Karen had been secretly certain he would look at his best, and when she first set eyes on him when she entered the drawing-room where he was talking to his aunt she knew — and felt her heart give a kind of wild leap within her—that she had been absolutely right.

The velvet doublet and the lace jabot, which were a part of the dress, more than emphasized his dark good looks, and the swinging kilt seemed to have been expressly designed for his lithe and graceful build. As he came across the room to her she saw the shoulder brooch glittering where it caught up his plaid, the falls of lace over the hands she had so often admired in secret, and the *skean dhu* tucked into the top of one of his stockings.

She did not know it, but her admiration was plainly given away by her eyes as she gazed at him, and Aunt Horry looked a little amused. She was wearing black velvet and diamonds, and for once she, too, looked impressive, and only Karen was aware of the inadequacy of her attire when apparently everyone else was going to be unusually splendid tonight.

She was wearing her one evening frock, which although it would have done very well for a simple evening, failed her altogether against the background of the Auchenwiel drawing-room, with its Hepplewhite furniture and its damask curtains. Or so she was quite prepared to believe until she saw Iain looking at her with a smile in his eyes, and to her astonishment she discovered that he was not even looking at her frock, of the same rather shadowy blue as her twin-set, but at her shining hair.

"You've done something to it," he said, puzzling over the transformation. "I don't quite know what it is, but it's different."

She smiled, with an immense sensation of relief inside her, but as Fiona came into the room at that moment, followed by Aubrey, she was spared the necessity of explaining that Aunt Horatia's own maid had washed and set it for her about an hour before dinner, and the finished result had amazed her, too.

At dinner she had Iain on her right hand, and once again she had that wonderful sensation of being protected and supported which was not hers when he was not there; and although most of his conversation was directed at Fiona, who demanded across the table a complete account of his recent travels, that did not seem to matter very much to Karen, who was happy because she was allowed to sit quietly and say nothing and just listen intently to the pleasant baritone voice of the man in the Mackenzie tartan.

By comparison with Iain, Aubrey, in an uninspired dinner-jacket, looked completely ordinary, she thought.

After dinner Aunt Horatia wanted to play bridge, but as Karen did not play she had to sit alone and look on at the others, which, however, she declared she was quite happy to do. Iain found her a large pile of magazines, and when he was dummy he moved over to talk to her, and even while he was playing he carefully watched the clock to make sure that the girl he was still inclined to regard as an invalid did not sit up beyond what he considered to be her most suitable bedtime.

Fiona Barrington watched him with a kind of open amusement in her golden eyes.

The next day, plainly to his disappointment, it was raining and blowing half a gale, and when he told her that he had planned to take her for a short walk on the moor and discover how well she was using her legs these days, Karen realized how much she had missed. In fact, as she turned to look out of the window at the driving rain, and saw the still bare-branched trees being lashed by the wind, she felt for a moment as if she had been wilfully defrauded of something quite invaluable, which it might never be her good fortune to enjoy again. She was so ridiculously disappointed that her disappointment must have showed in her face, for Iain laughed and looked at her in faint surprise and reminded her that there would be other occasions.

"I'll be over next week-end—if nothing prevents me And you'll probably be able to walk half a mile farther by then."

He was rallying her, she knew, possibly a little perplexed by her, and the one thing he did not know was that the space of time between one week-end and the next could be an eternity under certain conditions.

Before he returned to Craigie House on Monday morning he said lightly to Karen:

"Any messages? Anything you'd like me to say to Mrs. Burns?"

"Give her my love," Karen answered.

He raised one eyebrow.

"You really mean your love? Isn't that a little extravagant?"

"I don't think so," Karen replied seriously. "I'm very fond of her, and she's been awfully kind to me."

"And you make a practice of bestowing a portion of your love on people who are kind to you?"

"Of course not," she assured him, with a sudden rush of color to her cheeks, for his grey eyes were gazing directly down at her, and there was something besides amusement in them which she did not understand.

"Well, perhaps that's just as well," he told her, and then while she waited—wondering whether he was going to kiss her goodbye, as he had kissed her on arrival, although on this occasion there were no onlookers, and they were alone together in the hall—he lightly touched her cheek. His long, firm fingers merely brushed it, but it was a caressing touch. "Be a good girl," he said—as if, she thought, she was not much more than a schoolgirl—"and don't do anything you know I wouldn't approve of. By which I mean don't under any circumstances do anything to tempt providence, will you?"

Then he ran away down the steps to his car, but before he got into it he looked up at her and smiled a little mockingly.

"I will give your love to Mrs. Burns," he called out to her, and she stood watching until the long black car had disappeared round a bend in the drive, and she heard Aunt Horatia coming down the stairs behind her.

Aunt Horatia came up behind her and encircled her shoulders with a plump and friendly arm:

"He hasn't gone for ever, my dear," she said, and there was something humorous in her tone, too. "And be careful never to mistake gratitude for anything warmer than gratitude!"

CHAPTER TEN

SOMEWHAT to Karen's surprise the days crawled by, and the week-end came at last. It was followed by another week-end, and yet another, and by this time the weather really had improved. Spring was in th air—it was painting a picture all about them, a picture in many tones of green, enlivened by the pale gold of celandines and the sprightly mauve of crocuses. The little cascades coming down from the hills were running fresh and free, there were green patches amongst the brown of the moorland, and stagnant tarns reflected the sunshine.

Karen was feeling a very different human being from the one who had left London so many weeks before, and not only did she feel different but she looked different. The wan hollows in her cheeks had vanished, and her eyes were very blue. There was always a delicate color under her peculiarly fine skin, and the attentions of Aunt Horatia's personal maid had transformed her ordinary short, fair, curling hair into a spun-gold wonder that amazed her when she looked into a glass.

One day Aunt Horatia called her into her room and showed her some lengths of material that were spread out on her bed. They were lengths of gleaming silk, one in ivory, with a tiny, threadlike pattern of silver leaves, another in faintest cyclamen pink. There was also a huge bale of Harris tweed, with a delightful blue fleck in it, and half a dozen rich silk evening shawls spread out across the bed.

"I've been turning out my cupboards," Aunt Horry told her, declining, however, to meet her eyes, "and I've found all this stuff that I must have picked up sometime somewhere or other. It struck me that this ivory silk is the very thing to make up into an absolutely perfect evening dress for you, and I could imagine you looking quite enchanting in this pale pink."

She picked it up and made as if to hold it up against her guest, but Karen's clear blue eyes looked at her accusingly. She was not greatly surprised, for Mrs. Montagu-Jackson had been hinting so frequently lately that she would like to take her on a shopping expedition, offering as the excuse the fact that it was so long since she had shopped for anyone young, and that it made her so happy to see young things really well dressed.

"And as you're going to be my niece before very long, I don't see why we shouldn't have a wonderful time buying you an outfit—so what do you say?" she had asked.

Karen's cheeks had first burned with embarrassment, and then she had shaken her head fiercely.

"I wouldn't even dream of allowing you to do anything of the sort," she had said. "You've already been far too kind to me—far too kind!"

"Rubbish!" Aunt Horry had exclaimed mildly. She had not looked acutely disappointed but as if the answer she had received was one she had expected. "Well, we'll have to think up some other way of providing you with new clothes," she had concluded, with a sigh of frustration.

"I don't need new clothes," Karen had declared. "At least——" And then in a rising panic she had said to herself that the sooner the deception she was practicing was ended, and she was back in London, the better. She was being basely unfair to people who were good to her, and she would have to let Iain know her decision very soon. Now that she was quite well again there was no excuse for her remaining where she was. "At least," she had repeated, "I don't need them so badly that I'm going to let you provide them for me."

Aunt Horry's eyebrows rose, and she had looked at the slim figure of determination in front of her with a faintly puzzled frown.

"But you are going to marry Iain, aren't you?"

"I—I——"

"*Aren't* you?"

Karen had remembered the promise she had made to the man who had befriended her, and she had swallowed something in her throat, and then nodded her head.

"Yes, but we haven't discussed when we're going to get married, or anything like that. It's merely—merely——"

"Merely an engagement! Well, my dear, that's all it could have been as you've only just begun to pick up your strength after being so unwell, but talk of marriage is bound to crop up before very long now. And you must have some clothes to get married in. You can't expect a man to buy them for you until he becomes a husband, although I've no doubt at all that Iain would be delighted——"

"Oh, *no*!" Karen had exclaimed in horror. "I wouldn't accept a thing from him—not anything like that!"

"And even if you're not going to get married you still need clothes," her hostess had declared, with a return of her mildness, "and it doesn't seem to me that you earn enough to keep yourself alive, let alone buy other necessities. From all you've told me about that flatlet affair of yours in London, and the way you've lived, I'd never have an easy moment if you ever thought seriously of going back to it. And I'd see that you *didn't* go back to it," with sudden firmness. "Whatever happens about Iain, I'm quite determined that someone has got to do something about you in future!"

Karen had felt such a rush of gratitude—almost pathetic gratitude—to her heart that she had almost choked, and she could only mutter. "You're terribly kind!—you're far too kind!" and rush from the room.

And now here was Mrs. Montagu-Jackson with her ornate French bed entirely covered with costly silks and expensive tweed, and Karen realized as soon as she saw them that she had had a new inspiration.

"I've a dressmaker coming here from the village this afternoon—a really excellent dressmaker!—and I thought if you agreed with me that these would make up very nicely we'd get her to take your measurements and see what she can do with them," Aunt Horry declared, thinking with admiration that the pink performed miracles for her guest's delicate complexion.

Karen shook her head almost sadly.

"You know you're just trying to be generous again," she said, "and I can't let you."

"But, my dear girl, why not? If it pleases me? I'm tired of seeing these things lying about in my cupboards, and the tweed will get the moth in it if I don't do something about it. I thought it would make you a couple of nice skirts, and perhaps a big coat as well. It's exactly the tweed I would choose for you for a coat."

Karen's blue eyes filled slowly with tears. She wished she could make Aunt Horry know how grateful she really was.

"All the same, I can't let you."

"Then I'll send the whole lot to a jumble sale and be rid of it."

After that, of course, Aunt Horry won the day, and the dressmaker arrived to take Karen's measurements and carried away the lengths of silk, while Aunt Horry insisted upon Karen's accepting one of the silk evening shawls as a gift.

"You can wear it over that pretty blue dress of yours," she said, "and until the others arrive it will ring the changes for you nicely."

She patted Karen on the cheek, and said gently:

"You know, my dear, I do like having you staying here. You're so young and different, somehow, from most modern young women. And I want you to be happy. Although I was not at all sure when I first met you, I hope now that you really will marry Iain!"

Iain's visits at the week-ends were things Karen looked forward to with a blaze of longing in her heart. When he came, although perhaps he was merely friendly to her—even a little distant—she felt weak with relief because he was there. Whilst he was at Craigie House she was constantly worrying lest, perhaps, something might call him away—to London, or even farther afield, and that she felt she could not endure, although she knew that before long she would have to endure doing without him altogether, and that the sooner she was sensible and told him that this sort of thing could not go on any longer, the sooner some sort of peace of mind would be restored to her.

Once away from him—once *really* away from him—she would have to forget him. And when you know you've got to tear something by the roots out of your heart, every moment's delay is merely strengthening the agony when the operation itself takes place. She knew that if she had any pity on herself she would turn her back on Auchenwiel and Craigie with as little delay as possible and fly back to London, obscurity and work.

And perhaps if she worked hard enough at something she disliked she might forget these past weeks altogether. . . .

She made up her mind that the next time she saw Iain she would have this matter out with him, and explain that in her view the deception they were practicing had already gone on long enough. So far as she could see he was not in any serious need of protection from his former fiancée, although how he secretely felt about her she often wondered. Fiona was so beautiful; assured and a little mysterious, but apparently quite willing to be nothing more than friends with him now that at last she had come back into his life. To Karen she was quite charming, which seemed to prove that she had no secret designs on the man she had once proposed to marry. Sometimes Karen had the odd feeling that, if anything, she was a little too charming, and there were moments when the younger girl asked herself why—*why*, if Fiona was no longer interested, had she decided to make her re-entry into Iain's life? It should have been embarrassing for them both, especially as she had treated him so shabbily. But apparently it was not. They met and talked with one another as if they were old and well-tried friends, and were quite at ease in one another's company. Iain had been distant at first—perhaps cautious. But he had rapidly thawed, as any man must thaw beneath the appeal of those golden eyes and Fiona's desire to be friendly. And if sometimes the golden eyes rested on him, when neither he nor anyone else appeared to be aware of them, with a strange slumbrous, brooding quality that had set a warning telegraph working in Karen's brains, because she *had* observed it, it was really nothing whatever to do with Karen, as she realized.

But although it was nothing to do with her there was one thing she would have avoided for Iain if she could, and that was that he should once again become a victim of a woman who had already badly let him down.

When the fourth week-end arrived and, as usual, he made his appearance at Auchenwiel, Karen made up her mind that this was the occasion to come to a clear understanding with him. To tell him that the time had come to stop pretending, and for them to part. She simply couldn't go on accepting hospitality and kindness from his aunt and wilfully deceiving her at the same time, and he had to be made to see it. And perhaps once she pointed it out to him he would be glad to agree that the thing had gone on rather too long. He might even meet her half-way and suggest some manner in which they could terminate the affair without making it appear too obvious that from the very beginning it had been nothing more than a hollow pretence.

But Karen was glad she was going to have this weekend—it would be something to hug to herself in after days, and re-live wistfully when she could bear to do so.

On Sunday morning they all went to church in the big Daimler, and then after lunch she and Iain set off for their usual walk. At least, for the past two Sundays she had walked with him on the moor, and she found it an exhilarating experience.

He looked so well in his tweeds, and he never tried her beyond her strength. And he seemed to know just how much strength she had. It was not as much as she liked to pretend to herself, and the most disconcerting thing about her recovery so far was that moments of sudden exhaustion had not been altogether left behind. Those were the moments when he saw to it that she rested, and when, after a glance at her face he decided to turn for home. Those were the moments, too, when she felt that he had not given up protecting her, and thinking for her. They were the moments that were going to be the bitterest of all to recall when their paths had permanently divided.

CHAPTER ELEVEN

THIS SUNDAY afternoon the sun shone, and a lark sang high in the air. They trod briskly over the new green grass that was forcing its way through the dead bracken, and occasionally Iain looked sideways at Karen. She was wearing the new tweed coat Aunt Horatia had had made for her, and her shining curls were free to the wind and sun.

Whenever Karen also turned impulsively sideways and met the faintly perplexed, faintly amused grey eyes that were resting on her, she wondered whether he had recognized that the coat was new and that it was definitely not in the same class as her own cheap tweed, and whether perhaps she ought to tell him about his aunt's generosity. Then she decided that that could come later, when she made her appeal for a return to normality and all the appalling dullness that normality would inevitably mean for her.

Just for the moment, while they swung together side by side across the crisp turf, her courage failed her, and she was glad to give way to weakness and postpone the serious conversation that she herself had scheduled for that afternoon.

When they came to rough or uneven bits of ground Iain took her arm, and she wanted to shut her eyes and treasure the feel of his firm fingers holding her strongly by the elbow. She thought that if they could only go on like this through life—even if there were no Craigie House, and no Auchenwiel, and not very much money or the means of making life secure—then all the days ahead of her would be a kind of benison, and all she would ever ask for.

Once she did give way to weakness for a few moments and shut her eyes, and when she opened them again she caught him looking at her in concern.

"Are you feeling tired?" he asked.

"No—no——"

A cloud had swept across the face of the sun, and as the wind blew strongly in their faces it carried a few drops of rain with it. Iain swore softly, and looked around for some sort of shelter.

"There's going to be a shower," he said, "and you'll get wet, and it's all my fault. My wits must have been wandering."

Then they both noticed a tumbledown-looking cottage standing off the beaten track only a few hundred yards away from them. At first glance it might have been a shepherd's hut, or something in the nature of an outbuilding, but it was not. It had once been a strongly built grey stone cottage, and even now the roof was good, and the panes of glass in the windows were intact. There was a tiny unkept wilderness of a garden in front of it, and Iain took Karen more firmly by the elbow and led her up to the front door. When he turned the handle it opened, and just as the rain came down in earnest, driving in its usual uninhibited fashion across the moor, they were able to seek shelter in a small dark room which smelled strongly of damp and wood smoke.

Karen found her handkerchief and wiped the rain-drops from her face, and she shook them at the same time from her hair. As Iain looked down at her he saw that her cheeks were pink as a result of that hurried dash up the garden path, and her eyes were not only very blue but shining.

"Well, we were lucky!" he said, and looked about him at the humble interior of the cottage. That it had been recently occupied was obvious, for although it was bereft of furniture there was a wooden bench in front of the fireplace, ash in the grate, and a pile of wood on the stone hearth. He took one look at the wood and gave vent to a low, pleased whistle, and then he added: "Indeed, I think we were very lucky, for although this shower won't last long we might as well warm ourselves up while we're waiting."

And while Karen watched him he bent and filled the grate with sticks, and ignited them by means of an old newspaper which was lying conveniently to hand, and a box of matches from his own pocket. As the flame sprang up the chimney and the dark little room became irradiated with ruddy golden light he looked up at the girl and smiled at her.

"How's that for service?" he asked.

She smiled back at him. She was a little bemused by the suddenness with which they had been forced to desert the open and, until a few minutes before, smiling moorland, and find themselves in this modest abode which, although it plainly no longer fulfilled the functions of an ordinary cottage home, was accustomed to providing shelter for whoever it was who had kept the room supplied with kindling and firewood. And at the same time she was fascinated by the movements of the tweed-clad figure who had so promptly taken advantage of the facilities that were offered them and brought the little room to life with color and warmth, and watched him dusting his hands on his snowy cambric handkerchief with the awareness that her heart was thumping rather wildly, and that words would not come easily to her lips.

But he did not seem to notice this, although he did look at her rather keenly before he pulled forward the bench for her to sit down. And when she sat down and stretched her hands to the blaze, not so much because she felt the need of the warmth as because she was conscious of the necessity to do something with them, he took the vacant place beside her and observed:

"Although this house is empty and a bit derelict it's probably used by a shepherd, or someone of the sort, and I hope he won't feel very badly treated when he discovers how much of his store of wood we've used."

Outside the rain lashed against the windows, and the sky had darkened so much that without the firelight they would have found it difficult to see the outlines of one another's faces. But as it was, while hailstones bounced in the garden, and lightning ripped across the sky, and one or two claps of thunder filled the air, Karen was all too painfully conscious that the vivid flush in her cheeks was being observed with interest by the man beside her, and that he was indulging in an absorbed study of her expression.

"Sure you won't try a cigarette?" he asked.

She shook her head.

"No, thank you."

"I think you ought to cultivate a few vices," he remarked in an amused tone. "You really are a little puritan, aren't you? You hardly drink, and you don't smoke, and it's obvious you were very, very nicely brought up."

She looked at him for a moment as if she was not quite certain whether he was joking or whether he was serious, and then when she saw that there was merely the faintest suspicion of a twinkle in his eye she said to herself, trying to gather together all the shreds of her courage:

"Now—now's the time to talk to him! All that I've planned to say ought to be said now, for I'll never have a better opportunity. . . ."

And then as she still peeped at him timidly she saw that the twinkle had abruptly vanished from his eyes, and he demanded so quietly that he startled her:

"What is it you want to get off your chest, Karen?"

"I—I——" she stammered.

"It's been bothering you all the afternoon, hasn't it?" he suggested.

"Well, not exactly——"

And then once again his expression changed, and he leaned a little towards her. In the fireglow his eyes were dark and strange—there was something almost mesmeric about them—and his voice had a queer, mesmeric quality, too, as he murmured:

"Do you know that we've been engaged—in the eyes of a good many people, at least — for very nearly two months, and apart from saluting you in a chaste fashion on arrival at Auchenwiel I've never yet discovered what it's like to kiss you?"

And before she could draw breath to answer him in any way at all his arms were about her and he was holding her close—so close that she could feel the violent beating of his heart — and he put his fingers under her chin and forced her face up and covered her mouth with his own.

If his heart was beating wildly, hers behaved like a frantic mill-race once the moment of surprise which caused her to remain quiescent in his arms passed, and although his lips were hard and almost ruthless and seemed determined to draw her very soul out of her body, and her breathing seemed temporarily suspended, by the time it had gone on for several long-drawn-out and utterly unbelievable seconds a kind of shivering ecstasy was flooding her whole being, and she was clinging to him, and there was a quivering response in the lips from which he at last abruptly removed his own.

He looked down at her as she lay against him, as limp as if she had been dissolved into his being and become a part of it, and his eyes might have been black as he asked a little harshly:

"And do you still want to say all that you had made up your mind to say to me this afternoon?"

She shook her head. She managed to articulate the whispered word "No," and instantly his arms tightened about her like steel bands.

"Is this a change of front, or are you no longer in any doubt of me?"

She hid her face against him.

"I don't know what you mean."

"I think you do." His voice was almost stern. "I asked you to become engaged to me in earnest before you left Craigie House, and just because I didn't put it in a way that appealed to you you preferred to credit me with quixotic notions, and to discount altogether the fact that I was ready to let you tramp all over my heart from the moment you collapsed like a piece of thistledown in my arms at Inverlochie station!" He buried his face in her hair, and she felt him quivering against her. "Oh, Karen, Karen, Karen!—do you still believe that I want this engagement of ours to be nothing but a pretence? Do you still think I could let you go away from me and lose you altogether?"

She lifted her face. It was very white, and her eyes were enormous, and strangely luminous at the same time.

"But—but," she stammered unbelievingly, "you can't mean—you can't mean that you—that you——"

"That I what, sweetheart?"

"That you want"—she swallowed, and her voice trembled—"that you really want us to marry——?"

"I can't think of anything that I want out of life more than that," he replied, so soberly that she shut her eyes and wondered whether she was delirious. Perhaps she had caught another chill and her temperature was skyrocketing? Or she was dreaming a wonderfully colorful dream from which she would very shortly awaken! And then she felt his fingers gently stroking her cheek, and he whispered, very near to her ear: "And you? Would you still rather we went on pretending?"

"I made up my mind days ago that we'd got to stop the pretence," she whispered back, some of the torment the decision had filled her with in her voice.

"Because you couldn't bear the thought of marrying me?"

"Because I never dared to hope you'd ever want to marry me!"

His arms crushed her so close at this simple confession that they almost hurt her.

"Oh, my darling—my little love!" he exclaimed. "Why else did I so determinedly keep you at Craigie House until Aunt Harry whisked you away from me? And why was I so bitterly resentful because she did whisk you away from me? You must have known I didn't want you to go! That night when I rang you up you sounded lost and forlorn, and I wanted to drive over at once and demand you back. I think I very nearly did. . . ."

"I wish you had," she breathed into his neck. "But the sound of your voice that night was so wonderful I was almost happy afterwards. I could even bear being parted from you."

"Then you didn't really want to part from me?"

"*Want* to?" She looked up at him at last, fearlessly, and her eyes were like blue stars. "Don't you understand?" she asked very softly, as if she was dedicating herself to something that awed her more than anything in life had ever awed her before. "I love you! I've loved you, I think, from the moment you left the porter to look after your luggage and came across and helped me pick up the money I'd dropped!"

"And yet you said 'No' when I asked you to marry me!"

She smiled at him tremulously.

"I wanted so badly to say 'Yes.'"

"Sweetheart"—his mouth drew close to hers again—"I loved you even before you loved me! I loved you as soon as my taxi stopped behind yours and I saw you standing there, so badly in need of someone to take care of you! . . . I blame myself because I let you travel alone that night."

"You couldn't do anything else," she excused him. "We were strangers to one another."

"We're not strangers now."

"No," she breathed, and turned her lips to his.

Outside the sharp sudden ferocity of rain and thunder and darkening sky spent itself, the sun shone forth again, and the sky was once again a clear, spring blue. Inside the fire ceased crackling, and the little room became lighted by the first beams of reappearing sunlight, which found their way through the tiny window and made a golden aureole of Karen's hair.

Iain looked down at it where it strayed like a spun-silk cloud over his shoulder, and his fingers moved in it wonderingly.

"Do you know what we're going to do now?" he asked. "We're going to get married almost immediately and you're coming back with me to Craigie House!"

Karen's eyes gave away the fact that she had not yet grasped the wonder of this situation, or begun to be absolutely convinced that she was not dreaming. They were sitting side by side on the wooden bench before the dying fire, and his arms were holding her close to him, while his grey eyes were so filled with tenderness as they looked down at her that her senses were inclined to swim, but she could not believe that it was all quite real. She was too insignificant a person for anything as wonderful as this to be really happening to her—even Aunt Horry had been astonished when she had first seen her and tried to reconcile her appearance, and her lack of sophistication and poise, her lack even—or so it must have appeared to her at that time—of a dress sense, with the fact that her nephew proposed to marry her! He who had once been engaged to marry Fiona Barrington, possessor of everything Karen lacked!

It was the sudden recollection of Fiona which caused Karen to draw herself a little away from the man she loved with every beat of her heart, and to look at him with a struggling doubt in her eyes—a doubt which had to be dissipated before she could begin to be sure of anything at all.

"But are you really *sure?*" she asked, the doubt making her eyes look dark and uncertain, while he gazed at her with a glimmering of amazement. "I mean"—it was so difficult to find words to voice her uncertainty, but somehow or other it had to be voiced—"I'm so different—so very different from Mrs. Barrington, and you were in love with her once——"

"My darling child," Iain replied, very gently, "that was two years ago."

"Yes, but—you were in love with her, and I *am* different! I've nothing of her about me—no glamor, or—or anything like that! I'm terribly ordinary compared with her, and if I'd once loved a person as beautiful as Fiona Barrington I'm quite sure I could never love anyone else."

He smiled a little crookedly.

"Perhaps I wasn't as deeply in love with her as you seem to imagine."

"But you meant to marry her!"

"Yes; I meant to marry her."

Her eyes searched his face wistfully — large, shadow-haunted blue eyes that caused him to put out impatient hands and seek to draw her back into his arms. But she held him from her with determination, although the pressure of his lean fingers on her slender wrists was a little painful.

"Perhaps I'm silly, but—to me marriage is the sort of thing one considers only once in one's lifetime! And although I know it wasn't your fault that those early plans of yours came to nothing, two years is not such a very long while ago, and—and you could be making a mistake. It could be pity that you feel for me, couldn't it?"

"If it is, it's sufficiently strong to make me desperately anxious to have you for my wife!" with a hint of undisguised passion tautening the corners of his lips.

She drew a long, shuddering breath, and resisted the impulse to bury her face against him and cling to him with all her strength.

"But pity can be very strong sometimes. And I've more or less forced you into this position, you know. You feel that I'm helpless, that I want looking after, and I'd much rather—*much rather*!—have you recognize here and now that, as a result of all my dependence on you, what you actually feel for me is a kind of fondness—that I've aroused all your protective instincts—than that you should find it out later on, and realize that someone like Mrs. Barrington——"

He gripped her by the shoulders, and she thought for a moment that he was going to shake her.

"Have you noticed any overwhelming symptoms of my admiration for Mrs. Barrington?" he demanded, with a harshness that frightened her a little.

"No—no——" She shook her head.

"Or, if it comes to that, has it struck you that Mrs. Barrington has been affected by a return of her once declared passion for me? A passion which evaporated very quickly when she met someone else who was capable of arousing rather more in her!" in a cold, dry voice.

"No—no——" Karen repeated; but inwardly she could not be so sure of this. The emotions of someone like Fiona Barrington were by no means all on the surface—not even partly on the surface!—and to the younger girl it was impossible to imagine any woman coming in contact with someone like Iain Mackenzie and not feeling certain that the world would be well lost for even a portion of his interest.

"Then stop talking such a lot of utter rubbish!"

He stood up, and with his hands still retaining possession of her wrists he jerked her up almost violently into his arms, holding her so helplessly crushed against him that their two bodies seemed to become dissolved into one another, and the heavy laboring of his heart beneath her cheek was more reassuring than any words he could have uttered. She sighed ecstatically this time, and when once again he forced her face up and lowered his mouth hungrily down upon her own she yielded it with an eagerness there was no disguising.

He kissed her hair and her eyes, her soft throat and her cheek, and then once again her lips, and he whispered:

"I love you! There's no pity about it! I love you! . . ."

And then when he lifted his head he noticed for the first time that the rain had ceased, and the sun was shining. Karen, bemused by her own happiness, noticed these things also, but it was Iain who became instantly practical and recollected that they had a considerable walk before they could reach Auchenwiel, and if they were to do so before another spring storm burst upon them it would be as well if they refrained from lingering in the dark little cottage.

"I want to get you home without your being soaked," he said, taking Karen's arm and leading her to the door. But as she looked back at the small, bare room, with the embers of their fire still glowing in the grate, and the wooden bench still drawn up before the fireplace, she thought with a rush of half wistful regret that it was a pity to have to leave it. Ugly though it was, devoid of all comfort, it was the place where she had been happier for a short while than she had ever been in her life before.

One day, she thought, they must come back to it.

CHAPTER TWELVE

THAT NIGHT, AT Auchenwiel, both Aunt Horatia and Fiona sensed that there was something different about the attitude towards one another of Iain and the girl he had announced he was going to marry. It was not so noticeably different that anyone could have commented on it, but it *was* different. Karen had some strange luminous quality of happiness about her, and Iain's eyes rested on her very often. Not only did she turn pink under his look, but it was noticeable that she no longer avoided the direct gaze of his eyes as she had up till today. Indeed, once or twice Aunt Horry caught the two of them looking at one another so hard, and in so revealing a manner, that she said to herself: "Oh, ho! So things are not quite the same between them as they were! Something has happened!"

Fiona Barrington, in a cloudy black dress that seemed to clothe her white body in a shadow rather than conceal it with material, lay back languidly in a corner of a deep couch and watched them discreetly but often over the book she was reading. She, too, was aware that something had happened—probably out there on the moor that afternoon, she thought—and instead of appearing golden her eyes grew dark like cairngorms, and her silken eyelashes hid them broodingly.

No one played bridge on Sunday night, because Aunt Horry was a little fixed in her ideas about the appropriate manner of keeping Sunday, and they all retired to bed at a reasonably early hour. Karen, who received an extra affectionate kiss from Aunt Horry when she said goodnight, had already slipped into bed, and was sitting hugging her knees and staring with that same bemused look of happiness on her face into the shadows of the softly-lighted room, when the knock came on her door, and thinking it was either her hostess or Mrs. Barrington she called "Come in."

But it was Iain who entered. He was wearing his kilt, and the velvet doublet and lace jabot which Karen was certain became him more than they could possibly become any man who did not possess his sleek, well-held head and broad shoulders, his grey eyes with the thick black eyelashes fringing them, and beautifully shaped mouth and square jaw, to say nothing of his lean, graceful figure and slightly arrogant stride.

He noiselessly crossed the space between the closed door and the bed, and Karen instinctively pulled the bedclothes up about her slim shoulders that were only otherwise covered by a flimsy pink nightdress. But he smiled at her much as he might have smiled at her before that afternoon had provided each of them with some quite imperishable memories, and sat down on the side of the bed, reached for her lacy pink bedjacket and handed it to her.

"I know this is a little irregular," he said, his smile becoming faintly amused as he noted how swiftly she draped the bedjacket about her shoulders and huddled herself into it, "but there were things we should have discussed this afternoon which we did not discuss, and we had no opportunity to do so this evening. So as I was quite sure you wouldn't yet be asleep I decided to come along here now and talk them over with you. If my aunt saw me on my way she's not the type to think unpleasant things, and I took care that no one else should see me."

He reached out and lightly touched her hand as it clutched the edge of the sheet.

"How small you look in that big bed," he said gently.

"Do I?"

"Yes. Very small, and very——" Whatever it was he was going to say he changed his mind about doing so, but his eyes said all sorts of unspoken things to her, and she felt the color rising in a hot, revealing tide to her cheeks. He told her abruptly, "I've got to leave for London tomorrow."

"Oh, no!" Karen exclaimed, and so far forgot the unusualness of the situation as to reach out and grasp at his hand also.

"I'm afraid I must." He looked down at the small fingers entwining themselves almost convulsively about his, and then he carried them up to his lips and kissed them lingeringly. "That was one thing I meant to tell you this afternoon, only somehow—somehow we didn't seem to find much time for the discussion of ordinary prosaic things, did we?" smiling at her.

"No." But her eyes had clouded so much that there seemed no longer to be any light in them. "Oh, Iain—*must* you?" London seemed so far away—almost at the other end of the world—and she couldn't bear the thought of having to do without him now that at last they knew that they meant so much to one another. They had been together for so many weeks—even at Craigie House he was only a few miles away. But London! London, where they had first met. Where she had first seen him unloading his suitcases from the taxi. . . .

"I'm afraid I haven't any choice in the matter, darling," he informed her regretfully. "It's a business matter which must be attended to, but I'm hoping I won't be away for longer than a few days —a week at the outside. And when I come back we're going to be married without any delay whatsoever, and I've already told Aunt Horry all about it downstairs just now in the library. She's quite delighted to know that I seriously intend to present you to her as a niece, and she's promised to look after you while I'm away, and to begin making preparations for what she calls a 'suitable wedding.' I told her that we're not concerned with 'suitable weddings'—I'll marry you in the village church, and half the people of Cragie can come anr see us get married if they like, but I don't want anything in the nature of fuss or circumstance. Do you agree with me, sweetheart?"

The light had returned to Karen's eyes, and she found herself clinging tightly to his fingers.

The Arrogant Duke
Anne Mather
Cap Flamingo
Violet Winspear
Teachers Must Learn
Nerina Hilliard
Beyond the Sweet Waters
Anne Hampson
Get your
Harlequin Romance
Home Subscription NOW!
• Never miss a title!
• Get them first—straight from the presses!
• No additional costs for home delivery!
• These first 4 novels are yours FREE!
FIRST CLASS
PERMIT NO. 8907
Buffalo, N.Y.
BUSINESS REPLY MAIL
No postage necessary if mailed in the United States.
Postage will be paid by
Harlequin Reader Service
901 Fuhrmann Blvd.
Buffalo, N.Y. 14203

"Of course," she answered huskily. "I think I'd agreed with you over anything."

He smiled at her more quizzically.

"Even if I suggested carrying you away with me tomorrow morning and marrying you without any ceremony whatsoever? — probably in a register office? Just as soon as we could get hold of a licence?"

Her heart gave a tremendous bound inside her, and she gazed at him as if she never could take her eyes from his face.

"That," she told him, with a break in her voice, "would be wonderful!"

"But, nevertheless, not really practical!" He patted both her hands lightly and placed them within the protection of the bedclothes. "No, my darling, that wouldn't do at all, because Aunt Horatia would objectly strongly for one thing, and for another it wouldn't be fair to you." His eyes met hers gravely, and his voice was immensely serious as he continued: "I've made up my mind that the best thing to do with you as soon as you belong to me is to take you away from this climate for a bit—to somewhere where the sun shines more often, and where you can grow tanned and completely strong again. You're not yet a hundred per cent fit, you know, and I want to take the utmost care of you. Would you like to go abroad with me?"

"Oh, no," she surprised him by answering quickly, and contradicting a statement she had only just made. "Oh, no, *please*. Not yet, anyway. I'd much rather go back to Craigie."

"You would?" He looked surprised.

"Yes." A flush of earnestness overspread her face, and her blue eyes appealed to him. "I love Craigie, and I was so happy there with you, and I want to go back to it, and to know that I belong there, and that I don't have to leave it again—*ever*—unless I want to, or you want me to do so!" Her hand emerged and plucked at his sleeve timorously. "Oh, can't you understand? It was such a haven—such a perfect haven—and I felt so absolutely safe. I've never felt safe like that before in my life, and I so longed to see the garden when the spring was really here, and the summer. . . . And I thought that I'd got to go away—perhaps never see it again!"

Her lips were quivering a little. A wonderful softness overspread his face, and he murmured gently:

"Of course I understand. I understand perfectly."

"And you won't mind if we don't go away at once? Although it's wonderful of you to want to take me!" looking at him through the merest suspicion of a mist. "And really I don't mind where we are if you want to—if you really want to——?"

She was so afraid that he might misunderstand her yearning for Craigie House—which was nothing to her yearning to be with him for ever and always! . . .

"My little sweet," he told her, even more gently, while he sat looking at her in such a way that, although he did not touch her, she had the feeling that he had reached out and taken her closely and protectingly into his arms, and that his handsome mouth had actually pressed kisses on her face that was so anxious to receive them, "I want nothing that won't make you completely happy, and if you've fallen as much in love with Craigie as all that, then we'll certainly go there for a while at least. But we'll discuss all this when I come back, and in the meantime I mustn't keep you awake any longer."

And although her heart lurched unhappily when she saw him rise, and she knew that he had got to leave her, he stood up abruptly. His tall figure in the Mackenzie tartan and the velvet doublet and the flowing jabot seemed to tower for a moment beside the bed, then he bent swiftly and brushed the top of her shining head with his lips.

"Good night, my dear one — and *au revoir* for a few days! The time won't pass nearly so slowly if you remember that in a very short time now I won't be leaving you behind any more. And remember also that I love you—" He bent again, and she felt another feather's touch on the top of her head—"I love you!"

And although she put out a hand to stay him he turned away swiftly, and she heard the door close softly behind him, and knew that she was once more alone in the softly lighted room.

For a few moments after he had gone she wondered whether she was more unhappy because he had left her, or happy because he was coming back to her, and when he came back to her again they would not, as he had said, have to part any more! It was such a wonderful, incredible thought that it well-nigh took her breath away as she sat there in her luxurious bed, with her arms wrapped about her drawn-up knees, a bemused expression in her eyes.

She repeated to herself the words with which he had left her, and she wondered again whether she was awake or dreaming:

"I love you—I love you! . . ."

CHAPTER THIRTEEN

He had already left when she went downstairs the following morning, and because she had hurried with her dressing in the faint hope that she might see him again before he left, a sensation of acute disappointment welled over her when she entered the dining-room and found that his place at the long oak table had been vacated, and there was nothing but his empty coffee-cup and pushed-back plate to reward her for all her frantic haste.

But later that day the feeling of disappointment passed, and upstairs in her own room happiness returned to her when she sat before her window and looked out at the quiet view of hills and woods and the more distant encompassing wall of mountains, alive with color in the sunshine. For although she had got to endure this enforced separation she had all her memories of the day before to hug to herself—her memories of being held in the arms of a man whose very name made her whole body quiver like an aspen when she heard it mentioned, and whose lips had taught her that anything she had ever dreamed or imagined about being loved and in love was pale and colorless beside the reality.

The afternoon's post brought her a note from Nannie McBain.

She was back at her own cottage in Craigie village, and she was longing to see something of Karen. She asked whether the girl would have tea with her the following afternoon, and whether, if that was impossible, she would drop in and see her some other time soon.

Karen carried the note down to Aunt Horatia, and the latter said at once that, of course, she must go and visit her old nurse. Fiona was being driven in to Inverlochie by Aubrey Ainsworth the following afternoon, and they could drop Karen at Ellen McBain's cottage, and then pick her up again on their way home. That would enable the two who were linked by remembrances of Karen's childhood to spend at least a couple of hours together, and Karen was so pleased by the prospect and the opportunity that was going to be presented to her to tell her old friend all about Iain that her eyes glowed with pleasure, and she missed the slightly disdainful look which Fiona Barrington shot at her.

"And then you really will have to begin getting together something in the nature of a trousseau," Aunt Horry said, beaming at the girl whose expression was so openly revealing, and who was living just then, as the older woman realized, in a rosy glow of almost unbelievable happiness. One thing Aunt Horry loved was Romance with a capital R, and being able to assist it in every way she could. "I promised Iain that we would begin preparations without any loss of time, since apparently he's made up his mind to rush you into marriage, and as he won't be away very long that doesn't leave us with any time to spare."

Karen looked at her mutely but gratefully, and Fiona said in her softest and most attractive voice, "I can be of assistance to Karen over this business of collecting clothes, and I'd absolutely love doing so if she'll let me."

Karen still found herself mute—largely because she was not at all sure where the money was coming from to purchase anything in the nature of a trousseau, although she realized that she could hardly marry Iain while still in possession of the few clothes that made up her wardrobe at that moment, and nothing at all besides—but Aunt Horry exclaimed with enthusiasm:

"Why that's a lovely idea, Fiona! You have such perfect taste, and Karen is such a worthwhile subject to practise it on! I've no doubt between you you'll collect some lovely things, and that will make it unnecessary for me to go into Inverlochie, which I really wouldn't like a bit, because I hate shopping in country towns."

"I don't know whether you've made any honeymoon plans yet?" Fiona asked Karen in the same smooth, friendly voice. "But if you're stopping off in Paris, or anywhere like that, you can always add to your outfit with Iain to help you choose things—and, incidentally, to foot the bill!" Her golden eyes gleamed a little strangely across the room at Karen, and her scarlet mouth quirked upwards at one corner with a kind of dry humor. "But for absolutely essential things Inverlochie will do you quite well—it has some quite smart little shops."

Karen thought Fiona's voice had grated in an unusually sarcastic manner—unless it was her own imagination—when she added those words, "and, incidentally, to foot the bill!", and she looked with a hint of appeal in her eyes at her hostess. The latter gave a slight shake to her head, and waved a beringed hand in the air, as much as to say, "Don't bother about ways and means now, my dear—all that will sort itself out later on!" But Karen felt keenly that she was very much a Cinderella who was secretly despised by the beautifully-equipped Fiona—unless it was some faint stirring of natural jealousy because she had once been engaged to marry Iain herself!

And yet, in a moment, Fiona was smiling at her with all the sweetness and the charm her smile could contain — and usually did — and suggesting colors that were likely to become Karen better than any others, and materials that were the least likely to crush easily if she and Iain were thinking of doing any extensive travelling once they were married.

"And I think you ought to give yourself a rather more sophisticated hair-do," she suggested gently, while the topaz eyes dwelt on Karen's soft curls, "and perhaps a change of make-up. . . . There's an excellent hairdresser and beauty parlor in Inverlochie, if you'd like me to make an appointment for you? I go there myself sometimes, and I can thoroughly recommend them."

"And talking of hair styles, and things like that," Aunt Horry cut in, "I've made up my mind to give a dance for Karen before her marriage, for we really must introduce her to some of the local people. It will have to be rather a rushed affair, and the invitations sent out as quickly as possible, but I'm sure Iain will approve of my going ahead with the arrangements, because at the moment his future wife is a complete stranger to the district, and that isn't fair either to the district or to her."

She looked at Karen affectionately, as if she was anxious to show her off to the "district," but the girl herself was faintly appalled by the idea. Perhaps it was because she wasn't, as Iain himself had said, a hundred per cent fit, but she knew that she shrank from making new acquaintances just then, and being in any way shown off — largely because she was certain there was nothing about her to show off. And the fact that Mrs. Barrington considered a new hair style and a more sophisticated type of make-up might improve her was a clear indication that in the eyes of the lovely widow there was definitely something lacking in her appearance at the moment.

She wondered—and all at once her old feeling of forlornness returned to her—what it was about her that Iain had found sufficiently attractive to fall in love with? Making due allowance for the fact that beauty was in the eye of the beholder, she had so little of the genuine article compared with anyone as radiantly perfect as Fiona Barrington that to her forlornness there was suddenly added a little cold feeling of doubt.

Looking at Fiona, she thought, "How could he, having once loved her, love me? Or is it, perhaps, because I'm so completely different?—Because he didn't want to fall in love with anyone like Fiona again?"

He had probably been very badly hurt; he was probably afraid of beauty, and had decided that it was wise to avoid it. But that didn't mean he couldn't still admire it. Any man must admire beauty, especially when it was golden and flawless like Fiona's.

And the inference to be derived from that was that she, Karen, had something else — something different which had appealed to him! Her very forlornness, perhaps. He was dark, and strong, and vital ,and he had been drawn to her because of her helplessness.

But was such a feeble quality enough in itself to kindle the vital spark of love? It was much more likely to arouse pity, and pity was said to be akin to love—*akin* to love! . . .

She decided she must stop thinking along such lines, not only for her own peace of mind, but because Iain had told her that he was in love with her.

And to begin to have any doubts about his love would be to under-value him. . . .

And at least she loved him with her heart and soul and mind. There was nothing about him that she did not love.

The following afternoon, when she arrived at Nannie McBain's cottage, she was so looking forward to seeing her that all other thoughts had been temporarily put right out of her mind.

The big car, with Aubrey at the wheel and Fiona, wrapped in mink, occupying the space beside him in front, stopped right outside the cottage, and Karen had the feeling that she had had once before that eyes were watching them from behind the lace-curtained windows of the two adjoining cottages, as well as those on the other side of the street. Nannie opened the door just as Aubrey let in his clutch, and with a last, faintly regretful look at Karen—for unlike Iain he seemed to be quite impervious to Fiona's type of looks, and to find a curious satisfaction in the contemplation of those of the younger girl, whom he had already made several efforts to paint—gave his attention to the business of driving, and the car glided effortlessly away. Karen flung herself into the stout arms that were held wide to receive her, and within a matter of moments she was inside the cottage.

Looking about it she saw that it was exactly as it was when she had seen it last. The overcrowded front room still had its antimacassars and pot plants ranged along the window-sill, the highly ornamental firescreen and the huge family Bible on a little table in a corner that was also decorated with a vase of bright yellow daffodills. Nannie took her through into the kitchen, however, where a fire burned cheerfully in the shiny black range, and a kettle was whistling on the hob. A black cat lay asleep on the rug in front of the fire, a delicious smell of home-made gingerbread pervaded the room, and the table was laid with a lace cloth and loaded with a variety of edibles for tea.

"Now, sit you down there and let me have a good look at you," Ellen said, when she had thrust her visitor into a comfortable basket chair, and stood back to regard her.

Karen removed her hat and smiled up at her, delighted to observe that her old nurse herself looked fit and well, and was even more plump than when she had seen her last. She had been a widow for several years, but she was a very cheerful widow, who occupied herself with many things, and was always available if anyone required someone to take over a job of nursing, or helping with a new-born infant. In addition she organized jumble sales and whist drives, collected for overseas missions, and was a great help to the minister and the back-bone of the local Village Institute.

Just now she was determined to find out whether Karen had been properly taken care of in recent weeks or not, and decided that on the whole the answer must be an emphatic Yes, for although a slightly fragile appearance was natural to her, her eyes were clear and blue and happy, and there was a delicate pink color in her cheeks like the faint pink on the inside of a shell. She was wearing a beautifully made tweed coat which became her very well indeed, and her hair looked soft and well cared for, and made a golden halo about her face.

"Well, you look bonny," Ellen gave her opinion at last, when Karen was beginning to feel that the inspection was somewhat over-prolonged, "as bonny perhaps as I've ever seen you, for you were never one of those buxom lassies who can really fend for themselves. You were always a wee bit fragile-looking, and when I heard that you were ill I was well-nigh out of my mind with anxiety because I didn't know, placed as I was, what I could do about you. And then Mr. Mackenzie wrote and said that you were safe and being properly looked after, and it was aye a relief. The Mackenzies of Craigie are a fine family, and I've known Mr. Iain for years. Is it really true that you're going to marry him soon now?"

Karen felt herself begin to blush as she admitted that it was true.

"Then you must tell me all about it while we have tea."

The tea was similar to others Karen had enjoyed in that cottage in the past, but just now her appetite was not quite up to the quantities of home-made scones and bannocks, currant bread and crab-apple jelly, cakes and gingerbread with which she was plied; but there was so much to talk about that Ellen did not seem to notice that her capacity was more ladylike than it had been on her early visits. There were all the details of how she had come to meet the Laird of Craigie in the beginning to be drawn out of her by a persistent Nannie, and just how ill she had been, and what Dr. Moffat thought of her now. And when the wedding was to be, and where the honeymoon was going to be spent.

The large-hearted Scotswoman could not have been more anxious to hear all the details if Karen had been her own child, and as her eyes rested on the windflower loveliness of the girl in front of her a glow of pride appeared in them, and she observed that she was not really at all surprised.

"That you're going to marry Mr. Iain, I mean," she added. "You're so like your mother, and I used to think her pretty as a picture, although she faded, poor thing, after your father lost his money. She wasn't the one to stand up to shocks, but you've never led the sheltered life she led, and I think it's high time someone took care of you. And Mr. Iain's a man who can do so. Not only is he very well off, but he's the sort of man I'd have chosen for you."

Karen's heart thumped because he was the only man she would have chosen for herself, and Ellen continued, gazing at her more thoughtfully:

"But of course you're not a bit like that other one he was to have married—that Mrs. Barrington who's staying at Auchenwiel now."

"N-no," Karen stammered, wondering whether Nannie had recognized the lovely widow enshrouded in mink in the car that had brought her to the cottage a short while before.

"She was a beauty, that one—and still is!" the older woman observed, proving that she had seen her in the car. "And I'm surprised that Mrs. Montagu-Jackson has her to stay with her, considering the way she treated her nephew."

Karen crumbled a piece of Eccles cake on her plate, and Nannie exclaimed shortly:

"Almost as near to being married to her as he is to you now—that's what he was! And she broke it off—broke everything off at practically the last moment, as you might say, in order to run off with a friend of his! And if that wasn't the worst blow he ever had in his life, well——!

Her words dried up suddenly as the realization smote her that she was not being particularly tactful in the circumstances, but Karen reassured her quietly:

"It's quite all right. I do know that Iain was to have been married before, and that it was Mrs. Barrington he was engaged to. But at the moment she's a very welcome guest at Auchenwiel, and if there were any bitter feelings, well, they aren't bitter any longer!"

Ellen shook her head in perplexity.

"That seems to me more than a wee bit strange."

"And she certainly is beautiful, as you said," Karen added generously.

Nannie poured her out another cup of tea, and pressed her absent-mindedly to something more from the piled-up dishes.

"Beauty isn't everything," she remarked. "In fact that sort of beauty's a menace—it casts a spell over a man! Since you don't mind my talking about it you might as well know that Mr. Iain was so terribly cut up at the time that none of us would have been surprised if he'd—well, at anything he did! One minute they were driving together through the village, as happy and handsome a pair as you'd ever find, and the next—she was gone! And he just left everything and went off, too, abroad! He's only been back once until now in all that two and a half years, and then he stayed for about a fortnight and then disappeared again. We've often wondered whether he would come back and settle down at Craigie—perhaps find someone who would help him to forget. But I never dreamed it would be you, my dearie," beaming on her visitor.

Karen still toyed with the last piece of Eccles cake.

"Would you—were you very surprised when you heard about me, after Mrs. Barrington?" she asked, in rather a low voice.

"I was delighted," Ellen informed her, deliberately misunderstanding her.

"I mean"—Karen lifted her head and looked at her bravely—"we're so very different. You said just now that I was like my mother—pretty, and rather helpless—or I might have been helpless in similar circumstances! But Fiona Barrington is the most beautiful person I've ever seen in my life, and she would have made such an absolutely perfect mistress for Craigie. We're such a contrast that—well, you *must* have been surprised!"

Ellen looked at her with shrewd, wise eyes.

"Are you in love with him, bairnie?" she asked.

Karen's quivering, flushing face answered for her.

"*Very* much in love with him?"

The girl's jewel-bright eyes misted a little.

"Wouldn't any woman be very much in love with him?"

"The point is," Nannie answered, gently, "that he wouldn't have asked you to marry him if he hadn't been in love with you. So, although I'll admit it's not very nice for you having that Barrington woman staying at Auchenwiel just now when you're making plans to be married, don't make yourself unhappy by drawing comparisons between the two of you, because a man doesn't make the same mistake twice—not if he's wise!"

And although Karen was faintly amazed at the discernment of her old nurse—unless it was simply the fact that she had known Karen from babyhood—she was also conscious of a sudden sensation of relief, because a doubt that she had thought hidden in her own heart was dissipated.

CHAPTER FOURTEEN

THAT NIGHT she stayed awake for a long time because she had the hope, amounting almost to a conviction, that the telephone beside her bed would ring, and she would hear Iain's voice speaking to her from London. But it did not ring, and she grew so sleepy at last that she simply had to close her eyes and allow the waves of sleep to rush up over her, although her feeling of disappointment was acute.

In the morning she looked eagerly for a letter for him, but there was no letter. She decided that he was very likely a bad correspondent, or perhaps he was planning to return almost immediately, so she did not worry. But she was disappointed again.

But in the afternoon Mrs. Barrington ordered the car, with her hostess' permission, and suggested to Karen that she accompany her into Inverlochie.

"I thought," she said, with that warm and well-nigh irresistible smile of hers, "that we might make a start on some of your more urgent shopping."

Aunt Horatia had already made it clear to Karen that she intended to make herself responsible for the payment of all the things she required, and had overruled Karen's objection by declaring that she could look upon the outfit as a wedding present. Or if she wished to do so she could pay her back later on when, as Iain's wife, she would have money of her own—in fact, plenty of money of her own! But as this made Karen feel that she was mortgaging something that did not yet belong to her, and anticipating the benefits bestowed by a well-to-do husband when he was not yet her husband, she preferred to swallow her pride and express gratitude for such an extremely generous wedding present, since somehow or other she had to obtain the right kind of clothes for her wedding. She could not very well become the wife of a man like Iain with nothing but her present few possessions.

And in Inverlochie that afternoon, although, she was never quite at her ease in the society—undiluted as it was, since Aubrey for once did not accompany them—of Fiona Barrington, Karen really enjoyed her first taste of the more selective kind of shopping.

There were one or two first-class little dress establishments in Inverlochie, and Fiona knew exactly where they were situated, and how to obtain the maximum attention once she had entered them. Karen felt like a distinctly *gauche* and very young sister beside her, but the assistants in these various exclusive shops sized up her possibilities almost at a glance, and with the help of suggestions from Fiona the bride-to-be found that exactly the right sort of garments were brought forward for her to try on.

It was Fiona who decided that with her exceptionally delicate complexion and her light hair and blue eyes she would look well in a color she had never dared to wear before—a kind of apricot pink. An evening frock with a skirt composed of yards and yards of billowing tulle in this particular color, and a bodice patterned with rhinestones, was selected for her, and Karen could hardly recognize herself when she stood before a tall pier-glass and gazed at her reflected image. The apricot-pink sent such a delicious flush over her cheeks that she knew that for the first time in her life she was really enchanting, and the depth of her blue eyes was enhanced so that they appeared to gleam like the deepest sapphires between her long eyelashes.

Then there was a cloudy black net which did even more startling things for her complexion, and a gold lamé stole which added an exciting touch of sophistication and banished a little of her extreme air of youthfulness.

"It's a good thing to look young," Fiona observed, watching her with amusement as she studied her own appearance in the mirror with obvious amazement, "but when the man you're going to marry is several years older than you are it's not such a good thing to appear *too* young!"

And this was something Karen had hardly thought about before.

They spent another pleasing half-hour in a shop that sold wonderful twin-sets and glamorous knitwear, and here again Fiona knew exactly what suited Karen, and the latter allowed her to make all the decisions for her.

Underwear proved slightly more embarrassing, for combined with Karen's unconcealed appreciation of the delightful wisps of nylon and lace was the disturbing thought that these were really intimate purchases, especially the transparent nightdress, like the heart of a wild rose, which Fiona held up and admired, and remarked while she did so that she thought it looked exactly like Karen, somehow, while it was undoubtedly the very best thing to include in a trousseau.

When she saw Karen blushing wildly the look of amusement in her eyes grew noticeably, although at the same time there was something behind the amusement which for a moment caught and held Karen's attention, and she wondered how she would word it if she had to describe it to anyone. It had nothing whatsoever to do with amusement; it was withdrawn and cool and critical—and cold, Karen thought. And there was even the merest suggestion of contempt—or did she imagine it?

But when they went next door to the old-fashioned George Hotel for tea, and in the panelled lounge, in front of a brightly burning fire, shed their coats and scarves and made themselves comfortable in deep leather chairs, while a waiter brought them hot buttered toast and tea, her friendliness was so marked that Karen wondered whether after all she had imagined that look in her eyes.

Or it might have been a purely momentary flash of jealousy—something belonging to the past over which she had suddenly no control. For, after all, there had once been a time when she had concerned herself with trousseau items in connection with a marriage which was to have made her Iain Mackenzie's wife. And now that another girl was planning to become that wife she might occasionally feel slightly irked.

But while they had their tea she talked to Karen in the friendliest of tones, and was interested in all the details of this approaching marriage about which Karen herself as yet knew little.

"I think you ought to have a proper honeymoon," she remarked, when Karen explained that she was hoping to go straight to Craigie House after the ceremony. "After all, one only gets married once in a lifetime—or usually!—and a honeymoon is the reward for all the anxious moments that go before a wedding." She looked at Karen with her golden eyes, observing how readily she flushed whenever the actual subject of the wedding was touched upon, and how confused her eyes appeared at even the mention of a honeymoon, although some luminous quality in her face when ever Iain's name was brought into the conversation gave away the fact that she was deeply in love with him. "I think Paris is the ideal spot—or you could follow the sun for a few weeks. Wouldn't you like to do that with Iain?"

Karen knew that she would. But more than anything she wanted to go back to Craigie House with him.

"You mustn't let yourself be brought back to earth too soon, you know," Fiona remarked, inserting a cigarette in her long holder, and lying languidly back in her chair. A faint sparkle lit her eyes. "It's a little bit depressing, but even in the most devoted unions that moment of being forced back to reality does come, and it's a moment to be kept at bay for as long as possible. It's unfortunately true that when you climb the heights you can't stay there eternally, and that descent by the way you climbed is a trifle jarring sometimes. I found it so—but then perhaps I didn't marry the man I ought to have married! If you're sure you're marrying the man you ought to marry you may get a different result."

Karen gazed at her in a silence that was caused by sheer inability to think of any suitable words with which to answer her, and Fiona looked at her through a faint haze of cigarette smoke.

"It's all a process of adjustment, of course—but in some cases the adjustment is easier. I'm not sure that being terribly in love makes it any easier—it could make it a little harder!"

This time the attractive, soft voice seemed to drawl slightly, and Karen wondered whether it was purely her imagination, whether that faint sparkle in the golden eyes was now a shade malicious. But she still felt she was being talked at, rather than expected to join in a conversation.

"However, I don't want to fill you with any misgivings, and at your age you're almost certain to believe in the permanence of the happy ending. And this engagement of yours to Iain is rather like a happy ending to a romantic adventure, isn't it?" watching a cloud of smoke curl upwards. "You met in a train, and you fainted in his arms on a railway station, and naturally all his protective instincts were so strongly aroused that he wanted to marry you at once!"

She flashed a brilliant smile at Karen, and the girl flushed almost painfully.

"How—how did you know?" she asked, for she had confided nothing of what had really happened to her since she left London early in January to anyone save Aunt Horatia and Ellen McBain. She hadn't thought Mrs. Montagu-Jackson was the type to pass on a confidence of that sort, and Ellen had had no opportunity. Which left only Iain to do the enlightening and somehow it hadn't occurred to her that he would do that in very much detail to an ex-fiancée.

"My dear child," Fiona answered her softly, with a touch of archness in the raising of her brows, "these things get out, you know—and, in any case, it is terribly romantic that you should be proposing to marry in a week or two because you met one man on a train! And it's always the 'one' man, isn't it?— the one who makes the violent appeal? There's never any doubt about it once you actually meet."

"N-no," Karen agreed, gripping her hands together tightly in her lap. "I don't think there is."

"But the great thing is to make sure there isn't any mistake. Because a mistake is fatal in such a thing as marriage—because once you find out that it wasn't really 'the' one there isn't very much you can do about it!"

Karen felt suddenly cold inside. She disliked this conversation very much indeed, and she was wondering why it had ever developed along such lines. But Mrs. Barrington tossed the end of her cigarette into the glowing fire, leaned forward and patted the younger girl's hands affectionately.

"Don't look so frightened," she said. "You know your own heart, and we both know Iain—and he's the kindest man I've ever come across! Whatever happens, he just couldn't ever be unkind to anyone!"

That night, when Karen was lying in her big bed and feeling almost as if she was alone and utterly deserted in the midst of a sea of doubts, the white telephone beside the bed started to ring, and her heart gave such a tremendous jolt that for a few moments she was trembling too much to lift the receiver. Then, with the receiver to her ear, she heard Iain's voice at the other end of what sounded a very faint line.

"Is that you, Karen?" he said.

Karen answered in as faint a voice as the line.

"Yes—oh, yes!"

"How are you, darling?" There was a pause during which he obviously waited for her to say something in response, but her tongue wouldn't frame any words, and he continued: "I sat down to write you a long letter this morning, but somehow I didn't know what to say to you. Letters are so unsatisfactory, and I wanted to speak to you, but I thought you'd probably be out. And last night I was at a business dinner which dragged itself out for so long that when I got back to my hotel it was much too late to ring you. Although I was terribly tempted!"

"I wish you had," she breathed back, rather huskily. "I don't really expect I was asleep."

"My darling child," he exclaimed, "don't tell me you keep awake until the small hours?"

"Oh! Was it the small hours?"

"The very small hours!"

She felt, rather than detected, a laugh at the back of his voice.

"In any case, I was thinking of you until I fell asleep," she confessed.

"Were you?" The line had definitely improved, and the tenderness that swept into his voice was like something living which reached out to her.

"What sort of thoughts were they? Are you by any chance missing me very much? And have the hours been inclined to drag since I left Auchenwiel?" She realized that he was teasing her very gently, but the teasing note in his voice was something she loved best about him. And then the golden bubble of bliss in which this late telephone call had encased her was pricked by his next words. "I'm so sorry, sweetheart, but I shan't be back quite as soon as I thought—it may even be another week or more. But it's none of my choosing, it's something I must do whether I like it or not. But Aunt Horry has written to say that she's planning to give a dance as soon as I do get back, and in that case I think she'd better make it about the 24th, because I can more or less count upon being back in time for that. And don't forget you're marrying me very soon after that!"

"Am I?" But Karen's voice was edged with a disappointment so acute that he could not miss it.

"Are you?" he said, a little reproachfully. "It's almost all I've been thinking about ever since I left you, and if I'd known I was going to be away so long I think I'd have risked Aunt Horry's displeasure and brought you with me." There was a pause, and then he asked: "Are you remembering what I told you before I left?"

This time she answered swiftly and eagerly.

"Yes—oh, yes! Yes, I am!"

"And you'll go on doing so until I get back?"

"I will," she promised. "But I wish you were coming back sooner—much, much sooner!"

"My little love!" he exclaimed. "At least you don't wish it more than I do."

Then he told her that he must ring off because it was late, and he mustn't keep her awake any longer. She said goodnight to him with a whole world of suppressed yearning for him in her voice, and he told her cheerfully to start looking forward to the moment when he did actually return.

Then she lay down and tried to put behind her the memory of Mrs. Barrington's curious insistence that however much one was in love it was impossible to remain upon the heights of unadulterated bliss for long, and she wondered why it was that tonight for some reason she could almost believe that what she said was true.

Everything in life was so fleeting. Only a few nights ago Iain had been with her, and she had been living in a kind of wonderland of happiness because he had told her that he loved her. But tonight although there had been so much tenderness in his voice, and he had taken the trouble to ring her all the way from London, she was oppressed by the thought that he was not coming back for a week or more, and the oppression would not let her go.

And Mrs. Barrington had said that he was so kind—he was so kind that he would not willingly be unkind to anyone, and she knew that to be true. Then how much had kindness to do with his being in love with her? How much had pity?

She shut her eyes tightly and decided that she must go to sleep.

CHAPTER FIFTEEN

SOMEWHAT TO HER surprise, however, the next week did not drag itself out in quite the unsupportable fashion she had imagined it might do, because there were several more shopping excursions to Inverlochie, and at Auchenwiel preparations for the dance on the 24th were in full swing. Aunt Horatia was determined that it was to be an impressive affair. She surrounded herself with invitation cards, and got Karen to help her send them out. The big ballroom was opened up and subjected to a rigorous spring-clean which involved taking down enormous chandeliers and freeing them from every particle of dust, and the cleaning and polishing of mirrors and white paintwork.

Flowers were ordered, and wines and delicacies from as far afield as Edinburgh, and the white silk with the dainty pattern of silver leaves on it was made up into an enchanting evening gown for Karen, which was nicer when it was completed than either of her two new evening dresses bought in Inverlochie, delectable as they were. The white made the most of her extreme youthfulness, but it also gave her a slightly "untouchable" look, as if she really was as fragile as a piece of rare porcelain, and its lines were so simple that there was nothing in the least pretentious about it.

During that week, too, Aubrey made several more attempts to reproduce a faithful likeness of her, and one that he did in pastel was voted as really excellent. It showed just her head, and the graceful column of her throat, like a flower on a slender stem. Her eyes were enormous in the smallness of her face, and the faint wistfulness about the lines of her mouth was nothing to do with Aubrey's own imagination.

Aunt Horry declared that it was enchanting, and she was quite sure Iain would think so, too. Aubrey, who appeared really to enjoy himself while Karen consented to sit for him, declared in his uninhibited fashion that the portrait was one of the best things he had done, and there was a certain amount of regret in his eyes whenever he looked at Karen once it was finished, because she was such an absolutely perfect model, and if only she hadn't been going to marry someone else he could have fallen very deeply in love with her.

Fiona Barrington knew this. She supported him when he offered to drive Karen to her various appointments in Inverlochie, and if Karen hadn't been so preoccupied with other matters she might have thought it a little odd that Mrs. Barrington approved of "two young things", as she called them, being flung together, and was willing to forgo outings herself in order that Aubrey should have the opportunity of taking her place.

But, truth to tell, Karen was living in a bewitched world where nothing was absolutely real any longer, and many things passed her by that might otherwise have impressed her. All her thoughts were with Iain, in London, and although a hairdresser worked over her, and a beauty specialist did something to her complexion which made it hard even for her to recognize herself when she looked at herself afterwards in a mirror, and she started to wear some of her new clothes in order to grow accustomed to them, as Aunt Horry suggested, she had the strange sensation that she was not the old Karen March who had walked out of a London hospital and caught a train for the north of Scotland. She was a Karen March who was somewhat fearful of what lay ahead of her in the future because the promise of it was almost too much.

She was afraid lest something should happen at any moment to break the spell—the magic spell which held her at present and bound her to one man, out of all the other men in the world, who could make or break her, so far as future happiness was concerned. He who might have asked almost any woman to marry him, but had decided to ask her instead!

She was humbled and frightened at the same time because he had done so. Humbled because, in spite of her new complexion and her new clothes, she felt she had so little to offer him—frightened because it was like entrusting everything one held precious in life to the care of one person!

Nannie McBain, when she saw her again—and this time Karen walked to the cottage through all the brilliance and promise of a morning that was now throbbing with spring, and enough to arouse confidence in any heart, to lunch with her—did a great deal to prevent her indulging those treacherous fears which were no doubt largely caused by coming into such constant contact with anyone as physically perfect as Fiona Barrington. For without seeming to recognize the doubts Nannie talked a great deal of wholesome common sense, and it was certainly not her fault that a little witch-like woman of uncertain age, who was her nearest neighbor, and in the habit of popping in and drinking tea with her, paid a visit while Karen was still there.

This neighbor, whose name was Judith Drew, insisted on reading her tea-cup for her, after which she looked long and with strange dark eyes at Karen and told her that there was a ring at the bottom of her cup, but the wedding bells were muffled.

"You've got to be very careful," she said. "It's the light and the dark—the light and the dark who were made for one another, but who may miss one another altogether! . . . You may be caught up in a mist that will wrap you about—you won't see your way. . . ."

Her voice was thin and hollow, and her dark eyes seemed to be gazing at Karen, and yet beyond her. Karen felt as if a cold draught had invaded the cosy kitchen, and outside the sun had vanished behind a cloud. The monotonous voice droned on:

"You'll have to be very, very careful! You mustn't lose your way, because you might never find it again, and the mist is thick. There is danger in the mist, and—the light and the dark! They were meant for one another!"

Ellen's voice interrupted her sharply.

"That's enough, Judith! You're frightening the child, and anyway, I don't believe in tea-leaves!"

"It's not tea-leaves," the obstinate, hollow voice asserted, when a little of the vagueness had passed away from her expression. "It's all about her. . . ." And she gazed at Karen as if fascinated.

Karen stood up, fumbling for her handbag and gloves.

"I'd better go," she said. "If I've got to walk back." But she felt she was longing to escape from this strange old woman with the fatalistic eyes.

Nannie accompanied her to the door.

"Don't take any notice of what she said, bairnie," she urged, giving her slim shoulders a comforting hug. "She's a little bit funny in the head—we all know that—and she's always telling one or other of us something which could frighten us half out of our wits. But you've got no cause to be afraid."

When Iain did return very nearly a fortnight had passed since the morning he left Auchenwiel. He had sent a short note to Karen, telling her he was coming, and telling her, also, how impatient he was to see her. As he was not going to Craigie House he asked if a car could be sent to Inverlochie to meet him. Aunt Horry suggested at once that Karen and Fiona should go with it to meet him off the train, but at the last moment the wind swung into a bitterly cold quarter, and there was even a flurry of snow in the air. Looking at the darkening sky while safely protected by her supple mink, Fiona observed that it might be wiser if Karen did not accompany her.

"We don't want you laid up for your own wedding, do we?" she said, smiling rather strangely at Karen, "and Iain would hardly thank us if we allowed you to run any risks. And in view of your recent history don't you think it would be as well if you possessed your soul in patience for just a tiny while longer and remained at home here?"

Karen felt as if someone had suggested robbing her of something precious.

"Oh, but——" she began.

Fiona's smile grew faintly teasing—quite kindly amused.

"My dear child, of course you're terribly keen to see Iain, but we're looking after you for him, and I don't think it would be wise to let you go all the way to Inverlochie on such a day as this. We might have to hang about at the station, and—Don't you agree with me, Aunt Horry?" she appealed to her hostess. "*I've* got to do some rather important shopping, otherwise I don't think I'd go, either. And in any case I don't suppose Iain will expect us when it's starting to snow."

Aunt Horry looked at Karen with slightly more understanding eyes, and voiced it as her opinion that Fiona was right, so after that there was little Karen could say in opposition to both of them. But as she watched the car drive away from the front of the house and realized that she had very definitely been left behind, the disappointment she felt was so acute that it seemed to crush her for a few moments.

Then she went upstairs to her room to remove her outdoor things, and because she knew Aunt Horry always rested in the afternoons she stayed there, miserably glued to one of her windows while the storm clouds swept onwards and the afternoon developed into quite a bright and pleasing afternoon after all. At least, when the chauffeur-driven car came gliding noiselessly back up the drive a little after half-past four there was blue sky overhead, and every promise of a brilliant sunset later on.

Karen felt her heart do that wild suffocating leap which nearly always robbed her of the ability to breathe easily for several seconds, as the rear door was swung open before the elderly chauffeur could desert his perch behind the wheel, and Iain stepped out on to the drive. He was wearing a heavy, belted overcoat, and as usual he was hatless, and the sunlight that was becoming tinged with a warm redness bathed the back of his sleek dark head as he bent to assist Fiona to alight.

Fiona was laughing, and her eyes appeared to be sparkling, and there was so much warm color in her cheeks that she might have just returned from a brisk and exhilarating walk on the moor instead of in a closed car from Inverlochie. She was partly loaded with parcels, and Iain relieved her of most of them, while Karen stood rigidly before her window and waited for the moment when he might look around as if in search of her. But Fiona's parcels were unmanageable, and when he dropped one he had to stoop quickly to retrieve it, and his white teeth were flashing in his lean dark face when at last he turned towards the front of the house, with Fiona laughing up into his face.

Karen thought instantly how gay and attractive they both looked, and how perfectly matched. And as is someone had presented her with the means of looking backwards into the past she saw them as they must so often have appeared a little more than two years ago, when they were planning their wedding, and Fiona was a guest at Auchenwiel. No doubt they had done a lot of shopping together then, and he had carried her parcels from the car, and she had laughed up at him as she was laughing now. He had bent his sleek head down to her as he was bending it now, and inside Aunt Horry had waited for them.

Karen bit hard at her lower lip, and then told herself there was something wrong with her. Iain had returned and what more did she want?

She went to her dressing-table and looked at herself in the mirror. She was wearing a fine wool dress of a soft rose color, and when she had put it on directly after lunch she had thought it was most becoming. But now she was not so sure. Now she only knew that her excitement was making her shake at the knees, and it appeared to have driven all the color out of her face. Compared with Fiona's glowing loveliness she was a slight and somewhat sickly ghost. There was nothing about her to compare with Fiona.

As she went downstairs her knees continued to knock, although when she neared the bottom she felt she wanted to rush into the drawing-room and hurl herself into Iain's arms and cling to him—to pour out to him her thankfulness that he was back.

But she knew that in no circumstances could she behave like that with the eyes of the other two women upon her, and she walked sedately into the room—sedately and, obviously, with almost painful shyness.

Aunt Horry was sitting in her usual comfortable chair near the fire, with the tea-equipage that had just been wheeled in drawn up close to her. Fiona, her mink coat cast carelessly over the back of a chair, was lying back gracefully in a corner of a Chesterfield, and on the rug in front of the fireplace stood Iain. He had taken up the attitude male members of a Victorian household used to take up, his hands clasped behind his back while the blaze from the fire warmed him and threw into prominence his finely-held shoulders and his beautifully-shaped head and neck, and his eyes dwelt with a kind of complacent pleasure on the picture of the two women in front of him. Karen stood there in the doorway watching him for possibly a full second before he noticed that the door had opened, and then his head went up with a quick movement and his eyes looked directly at her.

Karen had longed so much for this moment that she could only stand foolishly gazing back at him, her blue eyes dark and intense and uncertain in her noticeably pale face, her pale lips quivering a little—for she hadn't bothered to add any more lipstick before she went downstairs, and she had bitten most of it off during the afternoon. Then Aunt Horry made a pleased sound as if welcoming her, and Iain took a few quick strides forward to greet her.

He placed his hands on her shoulders and looked down into her face. Desperation made her eyes darken still more as she fought to prevent herself from flinging herself upon him, and his eyes were quite inscrutable as they studied her.

He said gently:

"Fiona told me you were not quite up to the journey this afternoon, and she suggested you stay behind. How are you feeling now?"

Karen's eyes widened for a moment, and she looked towards Fiona—who was, however, complacently smiling at her. Aunt Horry was busily pouring tea and she obviously had not heard, so Karen remained silent for a moment and then answered in a strange, tight little voice:

"I'm perfectly all right. How—how are you?"

He did not kiss her, he scarcely touched her, but his eyes and his look were gentle and caressing—as if, she thought, she was so desperately fragile that anything in the nature of rough treatment might harm her. Then he put her into a chair near the fire, brought her a cup of tea when Aunt Horry had poured it out, and took up his position again in the centre of the rug, addressing his conversation to all three of them impartially.

Karen knew this was so utterly unlike anything she had imagined when he returned that it was as much as she could do to swallow even one mouthful of the hot buttered toast which was so plentiful on these occasions, and she all but scalded her throat through sipping hurriedly at her tea. But Mrs. Barrington lay back comfortably on her Chesterfield couch, and she was so plainly relaxed that Karen became more and more conscious of her own nervous movements. At the same time she was quite sure that whenever the lustrous golden eyes of the widow were turned in her direction there was something of a cat's smug self-satisfaction under the sweeping lashes, and behind it there was that subdued sparkle of amusement, too. And it was amusement in connection with Karen's own discomfiture.

The tea-time dragged itself out, with Iain giving them a humorous account of some of the things that had happened to him in London. Aunt Horry beamed up at him affectionately, and although the clock on the mantelpiece ticked away the minutes Fiona made no attempt to bestir herself or to think of dressing for the evening. Aubrey produced his pastel sketch of Karen, and it was duly admired, although Karen herself thought the admiration was a little perfunctory. Then at last Aunt Horatia said that she must go upstairs, while Aubrey returned the portrait to his temporary studio, and Fiona stood up with her languid, effortless grace and picked up her mink coat in preparation to depart.

But even then she did not depart hurriedly, and before she did so she looked towards Karen and smiled at her in a sweetly taunting fashion.

"I know very well what Karen is thinking," she said. "That I've had you all the afternoon, and now it's her turn!" The smile became brilliant, almost seductive, as it swept round to Iain's face. "So I'm going to leave you two love-birds alone together!" And this time the mockery in her voice was unmistakable as she vanished gracefully from the room.

CHAPTER SIXTEEN

When they were alone Karen felt as if the power to say anything at all had suddenly deserted her, and she was so overwhelmingly conscious of Iain standing near to her on the rug that she was afraid to lift her eyes to his face lest the expression in them betrayed her.

Not that it should have mattered—they had been parted, and he had come back to her, and her bones were prepared to melt into water at one word or sign from him. But the door had been closed for nearly half a minute before he spoke to her, and then there was something more like polite concern in his voice than anything else as he said:

"Are you sure you're feeling quite all right now? I thought you looked terribly pale when you came into the room before tea, and Fiona said you couldn't have stood the car trip this afternoon. Did you have a bad headache, or something?"

Karen lifted her eyes to him with a return of her astonishment, and she thought she understood why Fiona had made that excuse for her. Fiona had not wanted to be accompanied by her that afternoon, and returning with Iain alone in the car had been the first opportunity to be alone with him that she had deliberately made since her return from Italy.

"No—there was really nothing wrong with me at all, only—only it looked like snow——"

It sounded such a feeble excuse, but she had to say something. Fiona had already said quite a lot in an apparently convincing manner, and there seemed little point in trying to pin-point her as a distorter of the truth.

"I see," he said quietly.

"And Aunt Horry thought it might be best——"

"Oh, quite!" he agreed, with greater emphasis. "We don't want to risk your catching any more chills, and although I was disappointed I understood immediately. Although, as it happened, the afternoon turned out to be quite fine after all."

"But—you were disappointed?" She seemed to clutch at this like a drowning man clutching at a straw, and he was amazed to see the look of sudden eager hopefulness which swept into her eyes as she turned them up to him again. He crossed over swiftly to her chair and sat down on the arm of it, possessing himself of both her hands and holding them tightly within his own.

"Of course I was! Why, darling, I've been simply living for the moment when I'd be back with you again! You know that."

"H-have you?" But her lips was quivering all at once. She turned her face from him in order to hide it, and he could feel her whole slender body shaking with fiercely restrained emotion. But it was heaven, at least, to her to have him near to her again. "I wanted to come and meet you—I wanted to come and meet you so *badly*!—You mustn't have any doubts about that!"

"I haven't," he assured her, while his arms went round her, and at last he was holding her tight. "But all the same, I did think your welcome was just a little repressed—I wasn't even quite certain that you were glad to see me back!"

"Not certain?" She put back her head and gazed up at him as if this was the most amazing piece of intelligence she had ever heard, and her eyes were enormous and the dark pupils distended.

"Well, you didn't exactly hurl yourself at me, did you?"—smiling gently down at her—"and I haven't so far been permitted even to kiss you!"

"But I wanted to hurl myself at you!" She made the confession while her fingers clung to him, and her eyes implored him to believe her. "But how could I do so in front of your aunt and Mrs. Barrington? And I've been thinking all through tea that perhaps you— perhaps you didn't want to kiss me!"

"What!" he exclaimed, and she thought that his face whitened with the sudden intensity of his feelings. "Not want to kiss you when I've been separated from you for a fortnight, and craving to get back to you? What sort of man in love do you think I am?" And before she could draw breath he had stooped his head swiftly and she could feel the hard warmth of his lips on hers. She gave a little gasp of pure happiness and wound her arms about his neck, surrendering her own lips without any reservations whatsoever.

The kiss was the most satisfying they had so far exchanged, and at the end of it they were both pale, and unable to speak for several seconds. Then she felt his hand caressingly stroking her short fair hair, and he breathed huskily, close to her ear:

"So you really have missed me?"

"I've been counting the minutes until you returned! I was terrified lest something happened, and you were unable to get back when you said."

"Foolish darling." But his eyes were full of tenderness as they gazed at her. "As if I would have let anything prevent me! . . . And hasn't it occurred to you that I've missed you, too? Missed you so much that I could never even begin to tell you just how much!"

"Oh, Iain!" she breathed.

He held her so closely that for all too brief a while it was exactly as she had imagined it would be when he came back to Auchenwiel, and the feeling of hunger in the arms that held her corresponded exactly with her own craving to be in them. While he held her every doubt she had even entertained vanished like morning mist before the first warmth of the sunshine, and she knew that she was completely and almost deliriously happy.

And when he let her go from him at last for a moment it was only in order that he could produce something from his pocket which he handed to her. When she saw that it was a ring-case the breath caught in her throat.

"Well, open it!" he said, gently, beside her.

The ring-case was round, and of red morocco, and against the whiteness of her fingers it had a striking beauty all its own. But when she shakily snapped it open and looked down at the ring lying on a bed of velvet, the sheer beauty of the large and flawless opal surrounded by tiny diamonds drew from her another gasp.

"Somehow it seemed the only really perfect stone for you," Iain told her, while he watched her face, with its expression of unconcealed delight. "You're not superstitious about opals, are you? Because if you are we'll change it."

"Oh, no!" Somehow she managed to control the quiver of breathless delight in her voice. "I think it's absolutely perfect!"

"And you don't want me to change it?"

"Oh, *no*!"

Karen felt as if her heart swelled within her as she surveyed her ring—the first outward and visible symbol of their belonging—and when he removed it from its case and slipped it on to the appropriate finger of her left hand she felt also as if her heart missed a beat. The fit was so perfect that it was astonishing—although he admitted to her afterwards that he had possessed himself of one of her small gloves and taken it to London—but it was a purely fleeting astonishment, because he carried the slender-fingered hand up to his lips and softly kissed the ring.

"In a very short while now—if you're quite, quite sure you haven't changed your mind?—we'll have a neat gold band below that ring," he said, and the tone of his voice, and the look in his eyes when they gazed straight at her, turned all her bones to water. She felt as if she simply melted into his arms when he stood up and drew her upwards with him and securely into them.

"Oh, darling," he whispered to her then, "*darling*!"

The rest of that evening passed like a dream—a rainbow-tinted dream which might never occur again—and it was a dream of unadulterated happiness so far as Karen was concerned. She wore her cloudy black evening frock, and with the color returned to her face and her blue eyes alight with happiness, she knew that she was looking her best, and Iain's eyes seldom left her face. They sat side by side at dinner, and although Fiona sat facing them in one of her spectacular evening gowns it didn't seem to matter in the least, because under the protection of the table Iain's hand was continually seeking hers, and the pressure of his fingers almost hurt her at times.

Aunt Horatia looked thoroughly contented as always, and was full of the dance which was to take place the following evening. Both she and Mrs. Barrington had exclaimed over Karen's ring, and it was left to Fiona to remind Karen that opals were generally considered unlucky, and to express surprise because Iain had chosen one.

"But perhaps you're not superstitious?" she said, with the lightest tinge of mockery in her voice. "Or perhaps you're merely brave, and feel you can keep anything in the nature of unhappiness at bay?"

And it was only when she was lying in her own bed in the darkness of her room that Karen remembered, for no reason that she could think of, that Judith Drew, who was Nannie McBain's near neighbor, had told her that there was a ring at the bottom of her cup.

But the wedding bells were muffled! . . .

CHAPTER SEVENTEEN

THE AMOUNT OF trouble Aunt Horatia had taken to ensure that her dance was a success was well repaid. It was a surprise to Karen to discover that despite the apparent isolation of Auchenwiel large numbers of people lived near enough to have accepted invitations, and the drive was filled with cars bringing beautifully-dressed men and women to the brilliantly-lighted house.

Craigie, with its gentler beauty and much smaller size, was a fitting background for intimate small dinner-parties, and perhaps occasionally a very informal dance; but Auchenwiel, with its impressive panelled hall and staircase, its suits of armor and its portraits, huge public rooms and specially built-on ballroom, was exactly the type of house to provide a perfect setting for an occasion such as this. It was little enough used in this way, because Aunt

Horry so disliked anything in the nature of severe weather that she fled abroad to her Italian villa for increasingly lengthy periods. But tonight, although a light mist hung about the silent hills, and only a few stars showed through wisps of trailing vapor, the cars had come considerable distances, because a dance at Auchenwiel was something which everyone knew they would thoroughly enjoy.

Karen wore the white dress patterned with silver leaves, and she looked really enchanting with her shining fair hair and glowing eyes, especially as Aunt Horry had decided she was so nearly a Mackenzie that she should be permitted to wear a tartan sash draped over one shoulder which all Highland ladies wore on occasions such as this, and which served to emphasize the beauty of her white dress.

"I feel a little bit of a fraud," she said to Iain, when he took her in his arms in the quiet library shortly before the first guests arrived, and a kind of breathless excitement assailed her because the tartan sash which so emphasized her youthful slenderness was the same as the Mackenzie tartan of his own kilt and plaid. "I haven't any right to wear the Mackenzie tartan—at least, not yet," with an adorably shy upward glance at him.

"In a few days, my darling," he told her, resisting the temptation to crush her close to him and thereby possibly damage her dress, and kissing her lingeringly on the top of her head instead, "you will possess the right not only to all I am and possess, but to my name and everything else about me. Only a few days," sighing softly against her hair. "And then you'll be my wife!"

"Have you seen the vicar?" she asked, suddenly covered in shyness.

"Yes; I have—only we don't call them vicars in Scotland," he answered, laughing at her gently. "I've seen the minister, and we don't have to have our banns called, or anything like that, because I've provided myself with a licence which entitles me to marry you at a minute's notice if I feel like it, Miss March."

"But—but was that necessary?" she stammered, blushing uncontrollably.

"It was," he answered. "I don't propose *to wait* three weeks for you, my little love, and I think you know that!"

They heard the noise of the first arrivals, and then the orchestra which had arrived from Edinburgh started to tune up, and after that there was so much danger of the library being invaded that he kissed her hurriedly—although very satisfyingly—on the lips, and they left the library together.

Dancing with him later, Karen decided inwardly that if she had been born for no other purpose than to dance with him tonight in such a setting it was almost, if not quite, a sufficient justification for her existence. She was feeling so much stronger, and he was such a perfect partner, and the music was so tuneful, that for the first time for many weeks she felt as if happiness was a thing which could never escape her, and looking up into the face of the man she was to marry she felt utterly confident of their future together.

She might not be the kind of wife he should have had—she would not make a perfect mistress for Craigie, like Fiona, for instance—but she loved him with all her heart, and held in his arms like this she knew without a doubt that he loved her.

Afterwards she danced with one or two of the younger men visitors, to whom she was proudly introduced by her hostess, and with Aubrey, who was not really a very good dancer, however, and managed to catch his heel in the hem of her dress, with the result that he practically succeeded in ripping it off.

Fiona Barrington, who was passing at the time in the arms of a man who had paid her a good deal of attention all evening, paused and went to Karen's rescue, shaking her head over the torn hem and the clumsiness of Aubrey at the same time, and then leading her away to a far corner of the ballroom where she could inspect the damage more carefully. Then she said:

"You can't dance any longer like that. You'll probably catch your foot in that tear and fall down or something, so you'd better come up with me to my room and I'll see what I can do to effect a quick repair."

Karen was at first loath to trouble her and interfere with her enjoyment of the dance, although Fiona had worn an expression ever since dinner which suggested that she was not greatly enjoying herself. However, she gave in, and Fiona led the way up the broad staircase to her room, and there brought out a work-box and a needle and thread.

"Just a few stitches," she said, "and at least you'll be able to continue dancing. Iain would hardly enjoy his evening if you had to fall out, would he?" looking at her a trifle dryly.

Karen thanked her, and hoped that they might return downstairs as quickly as possible, but Fiona seemed in no hurry—in fact, she seemed very much the reverse, and after tacking the hem up again she suggested that as it was very hot downstairs, and very cool where they were, and that Iain, in any case, had a few duty dances to perform, they might as well enjoy a few moments of respite.

"Sit down," she said, "and have a cigarette."

She pushed a comfortable chair towards Karen and took another herself, then produced an exquisite toy of a gold and enamel cigarette-case from her evening bag and offered it to the younger girl. Karen so seldom smoked that she would have preferred to decline, but she thought at once that this might cause Fiona's lovely sleek eyebrows to lift a little in amusement because of her lack of sophistication, and so she accepted one instead.

She had already observed that the bedroom was very similar to her own, but it was filled with so many of Fiona's own costly things that it looked extremely luxurious. The bed was already turned down, and there was Fiona's nightdress — an exquisite froth of transparent peach-colored georgette —laid out ready for her across it. Fiona's black satin house-coat lay across the foot of the bed, and a pair of tiny velvet mules were placed ready for her to step into.

The dressing-table was loaded with cosmetics and various gold-stoppered bottles and flagons, as well as magnificent gold-backed hairbrushes and a handmirror. A photograph in a neat but expensive-looking frame occupied a prominent position amongst the various toilet articles, and as the room was flooded with soft but brilliant light it was easy enough for Karen to recognize the face of the man who seemed to be looking straight towards her.

She sat almost bolt upright in her chair as she recognized Iain, and Mrs. Barrington, lying languidly back in her own chair, smiled a slow, appreciative smile.

"Ah, I see you have caught sight of Iain's photograph!" she exclaimed.

Karen looked at her as if she was seeking an explanation, and then back at the handsome, faintly smiling face of the man she was to marry. The photograph had probably been taken three or four years before, but it was Iain as she knew him—and loved him!

"Are you so very surprised to see that I treasure his photograph?" Fiona demanded softly.

"I don't think I quite understand," Karen began. "I mean—I know, of course, that you were once engaged to be married——"

"Just as you are at the present time," Fiona murmured, as if the thought amused her. "You're going to marry Iain now—and I was going to marry him two years ago. But I made a mistake and let him go, and of course I lived to realize how wrong I was! You may live to do just that very thing, and that's why I thought it would be a very good plan to remain up here for a little while and have a little talk with you instead of rushing back to the dancers. One can dance at almost any time if one seriously wants to, but once one's made a bad mistake like rushing into an unwise marriage it isn't so easy to extricate oneself."

"I still don't think I understand," Karen managed to articulate, very softly, and the other woman smiled pleasantly.

"My dear girl, that's because you're young, and at the moment you think you're in love—but are you *quite* sure Iain's in love with you?"

"I—" Karen put a hand up to her throat, as if she felt a tightness there—"I—You've said yourself that we're going to be married!"

"Yes, of course you are, my dear—or you will be, if you feel like going through with it. But what I asked you was—*is* Iain in love with you? Not just temporarily carried away because you're so young and helpless, and he happens to be the type of man to whom helpless creatures appeal! I think I told you once before that he's terribly kind, and you more or less put him into the position where he hadn't much choice but to ask you to marry him, didn't you?" Her smile remained pleasant, and even sympathetic. "Oh, my dear, I understand perfectly. He's terribly attractive, and you couldn't say 'no' when he asked you, of course."

Karen found that she was voiceless. Inside her she had gone very cold, and something was still and waiting deep down amongst the roots of her being—waiting for the moment when everything she valued most would be wrenched away from her.

"Listen!" Fiona leant a little towards her. "Shall I tell you the truth about Iain and myself?" As Karen made no attempt to answer she continued: "We adored one another years ago, and I adore him still. I married another man because he was wealthier than Iain, and because I was a fool. But the moment I was free I wrote to Iain and told him I wanted us to meet again, and he agreed it was the only sensible thing to do. Because when two people have been so deeply in love that they know they can never experience anything like it again they can't afford to let pride stand in the way! And Iain had already wandered unhappily about the world for nearly two years because of me. So when his aunt asked me to stay with her I thought it a splendid idea, and Iain would have thought it a splendid idea—but for you!"

Her golden eyes flickered, as if she was endeavoring to keep reproach and hostility out of them, but finding it difficult.

"If he hadn't run into you on that night train to Edinburgh, and taken you to Craigie House—where he *had* to say something to prevent gossip arising, and thought up that story about an engagement—he and I would now be preparing for the wedding that should have taken place two years ago, and *you* wouldn't be any the worse off, would you? Because you would never have known him!"

"And what do you want me to do?" Karen asked, in a strangely quiet, controlled, and rather weary voice.

"My dear child, I don't want you to do anything dramatic. But just think, before you take the very final step of marrying Iain, whether it really is the wisest and most sensible step you could take! Ask yourself what there is about you that could hold a man like Iain for long, even if something about you appeals strongly to him at the moment! Ask yourself how you'll feel when it becomes obvious that he's losing interest a little—that he's resenting being tied— that he's resenting losing *me*! Because I can assure you he's never stopped loving me—not deep down in his heart!"

She crushed out the end of her cigarette in an ashtray, and then carefully selected another, stuck it in the end of her long turquoise holder and lighted it. She looked at Karen carefully and consideringly.

"I've known all along that you don't actually *believe* in his love for you," she told her. "It's been in your face at times—that nagging doubt! And so do please think this thing over very carefully before you take that final step, not only for your own sake, but for the sakes of all three of us!"

Then, although she had only just lighted the fresh cigarette, she crushed it out in the ashtray and rose gracefully.

"Perhaps we'd better get back to the others now," she said, "or our absence will begin to be noticed."

Karen got through the remainder of that evening without noticeably betraying the fact that there was no longer any enjoyment in it for her, and when at last Iain remarked that she looked tired she explained that she had given her ankle a slight wrench, and it was hurting a little.

It was close upon three o'clock in the morning, and already there was a slight thinning of the guests. She decided that it would not be unreasonable to plead a desire to go to bed.

"If you'd explain to Aunt Horry that I'm tired," she said, looking up into his face with large but quite unrevealing eyes. She smiled faintly. "This sort of thing is new to me, you know," she added. "I'm not accustomed to exciting dissipations of this sort."

"Of course, darling," he answered, and drew her into the quiet hall and to the foot of the handsome carved staircase. There he kissed her gently, but lingeringly, on her slightly drooping lips. "Don't you bother about Aunt Horry—she'll understand. And I think you can do with some sleep."

He stood watching her until she reached the bend in the stairs which took her out of his sight, and even after that she had the feeling that he was still standing and looking upwards at the spot where she had disappeared.

In her own room she not only shut the door but locked it, because it provided her with a feeling of inviolability which was important to her just then. She could not have borne it if Aunt Horry had sent someone to help her into bed, or to bring her hot milk, or something of the sort. And she simply could not have endured it if Fiona Barrington had come along to have any more conversation with her.

She sat on the side of her bed and remembered the words Judith Drew had used to her on the afternoon which now seemed centuries ago. "You've got to be very careful," Judith had said, "but it's the dark and the light — the dark and the light, who were made for one another, and who may miss one another altogether! . . . You may be caught up in a mist that will wrap you about—you won't see your way. . . ."

But Karen was seeing her way all too clearly. In fact, it was the only possible way ahead of her, and at the bottom of her heart she had known this for weeks. Fiona Barrington was right when she said that there was nothing about Karen to hold a man like Iain—in fact, the only really amazing thing was that he had ever been attracted to her at all. And, of course, he hadn't, really. It had been pity in the beginning, and now he probably felt responsible for her, and at all costs he was determined to go through with this idea of marrying her because she had already shown how little she was capable of looking after herself.

But, in time, the tie between them would pall abominably, and also he would have lost Fiona for the second time. Just now he might be feeling sore with Fiona—secretly willing to punish her—but when he awoke to the full realization that by his own act he had put another barrier between them, he was almost certain to be horrified by what he had done. And by that time it would be too late!

Karen, viewing the whole matter as calmly and dispassionately as if she had never had any feelings whatsoever, and was incapable of even a twinge of self-pity—odd though it was, she felt rather like something that had been cast up by the tide, and without enough energy to be vitally concerned about anything so purely personal as her own interests—knew that there was only one thing for her to do, and she was going to do it.

She went to her window and looked out. The stars still seemed to be shining thinly through a curtain of mist. There were hardly any cars left in the drive, the music of the orchestra had died away, and the house itself was becoming very silent.

She slipped out of her lovely white evening gown and the tartan sash that had filled her with so much pride all evening, and putting on a dressing-gown lay down on the outside of her bed to wait until the house was completely silent, and the daylight was not far away. Her wrist-watch said four o'clock, which meant she had another full hour, and more, before dawn began to break. But in the interval she did not dare to close her eyes, even if she felt like sleep—which she did not!—and as soon as the first faintly greyish light began to steal in through her windows she slipped like a shadow from the bed and started to dress feverishly.

She would have to leave all her things behind—but that didn't matter, because they were not really her things. Only the heavy tweed coat which Aunt Horry had had made for her she decided to wear, as a protection for one thing against the raw chill of the morning, but chiefly because Aunt Horry *had* had it made for her, and it would be something belonging to these past few weeks that she could keep and treasure.

She felt that the writing of a note to leave behind her was a gesture which she disliked because of the drama which clung to it, but it had to be done because no one must suffer any anxiety on her account, and minds had to be set at rest. The letter (addressed to Aunt Horry and not to Iain) said simply that she had made up her mind to leave because after much thought she was certain it was the wisest course, and offered thanks to her hostess for all that she had done for her. Then she placed it in a prominent position on the dressing-table and turned to leave.

She spared herself that last look round the room, with its security and its comforts, which might have caused her to weaken, and because she was so anxious that no one should be disturbed by her departure or attempt to prevent it she took off her shoes and carried them until she reached the bottom of the wide staircase.

The hall was almost in complete darkness, because as yet the dawn light had not found its way into it, and she did not dare to switch on any electric light in order to unfasten the great front door. This meant that she had to fumble in the gloom with latches and bolts, tugging at them breathlessly, and with fear in her heart lest someone should overhear and appear at the top of the staircase.

But no one did overhear, and the bolts were kept so well oiled that, despite their cumbersomeness, after a few moments they yielded to her tugs, and the front door at last opened so suddenly that it took her a little by surprise.

The cold, dank air of a misty March morning rushed in and past her face, and she shivered a little after the warmth of the hall. But in a moment she was outside, her breathing not quite so agonized, the rawness and the coldness causing her to forget for a moment the urgency of all this.

And then she closed the door silently behind her. Spirals of cotton-wool-like vapor drifted towards her, wreathing about her like gossamer scarves, and she realized that it would probably be very misty out on the moor. But she had only to cross a very small portion of it in order the reach the village and Nannie McBain's house. And once at Nannie McBain's the only thing she had to do was to persuade her old nurse somehow or other to get a taxi that would take her to the station at Inverlochie.

CHAPTER EIGHTEEN

BUT ALTHOUGH SHE was certain that by this time she knew fairly well the portion of moor she had to cross, having walked on it most days when it was fine, it was astonishing how a thin curtain of mist could give it an entirely different appearance. And in places the mist was not so thin—in fact, there were pockets where it was quite thick. Karen's first indication that she might not be following the right path was received when she found herself near the edge of a reed-fringed pond, which was certainly not normally encountered on a walk to the village.

The pond looked dark and stagnant in the eerie grey light, and the reeds bending back from it were brown as yet. Karen turned away hurriedly, and found herself confronted by a couple of moorland sheep that looked positively enormous as they loomed up in front of her. She heard a frightened bleat, and then both the sheep bounded away, and once again she was alone and now all but hemmed in by a cloying blanket of dense white mist.

She wasn't really alarmed at first, because she felt sure that if she kept on walking she would be bound to arrive in the midst of another comparatively clear patch before long, when she could take her bearings and look for something familiar, such as the cairn of stones she had passed so often, or the sudden steep declivity in the ground at the foot of which was a shepherd's hut, protected from the prevailing wind.

Whether it was because she had already arrived on lower ground, she could not tell, but the mist grew thicker with every step she took, and at last she felt certain that she was going round in circles, because she again came up against the edge of the pond after keeping moving for about a quarter of an hour. Even then she was not really alarmed, because the mist must thin as the sun rose higher in the sky—or so, in her ignorance of that part of the world, she thought.

But after walking for another half an hour and arriving nowhere she began to be aware of an uneasy cold feeling inside her, and to realize that she had behaved in the stupidest manner possible, rushing out into the early light without paying any real heed to the weather, or giving a thought to the fact that these were the Scottish Highlands. For all she knew to the contrary the moor might go on indefinitely, and even if it didn't, in this blanketing mist her hopes of finding herself suddenly back upon the road were probably dim in the extreme.

She was also vexed to the point of tears because once again she had proved herself incapable of arriving at the end of a journey she had set out to accomplish without help from anyone else. She had left London without much thought when she was still quite unfit for travel and had involved Iain in all sorts of unnecessary complications because of her very lack of thought, and that should at least have been a lesson to her. But now, unless she was very lucky, there was no one about who could help her, and if the midst remained obstinate and refused to lift, how on earth was she going to get to Nannie McBain's cottage?

She recalled scraps of conversation she had listened to at various times—even as far back as the times she had stayed with Ellen McBain—to the effect that the mist sometimes hung about the mountain tops for days, so why should it not linger here on the moor, which, after all, was a considerable distance above sea level?

In desperation she pressed on, realizing that but for the thickness of her good tweed coat she would be shivering uncontrollably, and that already her hair was wet through and clinging in soaking tendrils to her brow and at the back of her neck. She began to be so tired, too, that she longed to sit down on every hummock of grass she came across, but she knew that one of the surest ways to catch another chill was to sit down for any length of time in her cold, wet state on ground that would be even more wet. And as, once she sat down, she might not find it so easy to drag herself to her feet again, she fought against her weaker inclinations and kept on.

She might not have been quite so easily exhausted, she realized, if she had had some breakfast inside her before she started off, having had nothing to eat since dinner the previous night — for Fiona Barrington had spoiled any appetite she might have had for the wonderful cold supper which had been served soon after midnight—and it was now, by her watch, very nearly ten o'clock.

She had been wandering on the moor for over three hours!

It seemed to her incredible. She was also feeling a little vague about things generally. She kept seeing vivid mental pictures of Iain, fresh and shaved and alert in his well-cut tweeds, on his way down to breakfast at Auchenwiel, and Fiona joining him at the well-loaded table. He would help her to dishes from the sideboard, and she, too, would be wearing beautifully-cut tweeds, and perhaps a gold charm bracelet on her slender wrist, and pearl studs in her shapely, shell-like ears. And probably neither of them was yet aware that Karen was not in her room, because the maid might have thought she was sleeping late when she did not answer her knock, and left her undisturbed. People did sleep late after a dance which had kept them up and presumably enjoying themselves until the small hours, and only the Mrs. Barringtons of this world were possessed of the amount of energy to rise in time to join the one man who most interested them at the breakfast table.

It was girls like Karen, who had been ill, and who were cosseted in case they should become ill again, who were a nuisance to other people because of the amount of care it was necessary to expend on them, and who would make a man like Iain feel that he had been unfairly trapped into marriage if the life-guardianship of such a girl should fall to his lot.

Karen found that she was stumbling a little as she forced herself to go forward, and she began to long almost feverishly for the power to pierce the endless wall of mist with her straining eyes.

Then at last, she came up against something new—or it was new when she first caught sight of it, and found herself leaning partly over it. It was a fence, and as the mist was playing one of those tricks when it pretended to thin she could see that it enclosed some sort of a wild and tangled garden—the garden of a cottage!

Feverishly, not daring to hope, she felt her way along the fence until she came to a tiny, swinging, open gate, and passing through it, she soon discovered she was on a hard brick path which led straight to a front door, looking like a hollow cavity in the mist as she gazed at it. And then, when she reached the door, exhausted though she was, and well-nigh sobbing as a result of her fear that the cottage might dissolve into nothing but a kind of mirage, she knew that she recognized the door and that the entire front of the cottage—or as much as could be seen of it—was also familiar to her. She had seen it for the first time on a Sunday afternoon about a couple of weeks before, and for that reason alone it was the most blessedly familiar cottage she could never have come upon. It meant that at least she was no longer lost, and that inside, unless the door was locked, there would be shelter for her.

But the door was not locked. It yielded to her touch just as it had yielded to Iain on that golden Sunday afternoon, and inside it was just as empty as it had been then, with the bench before the fire, although there was no little pile of kindling and faggots on the stone hearth waiting and ready to be coaxed into a blaze.

But the bench was the most welcome sight Karen had seen for a long time, and she staggered towards it and dropped down on it with the knowledge that after another quarter of an hour out there on the moor she would not have had the strength to reach it. She would probably have fallen in her tracks and become so numbed with the cold and the misery of it all that anything might have happened to her. But, as it was, she was safe again—safe from the risk of exposure, from the frightening desolation of the moor and the horror of being lost on it, and safe from the nightmare of keeping moving in a world where everything around her was still and dark.

By degrees, as she sat there, her exhaustion passed sufficiently for her to realize even more keenly than she had done how much she had been spared. For even if the mist did not disperse for another twenty-four hours, at least she would be able to find her way back when it did lift, and in the meantime she had a roof over her head, and four stout walls to enclose her.

After a time she began to look about her, and saw that there was another door which probably led to a small back room. When she penetrated into that room she found that it was hardly more than a store room, but inside it was a decrepit oil stove, with a box of matches on a shelf.

On hands and knees she discovered thankfully that the stove did work, and also that it was filled with oil—whoever used the cottage was plainly in the habit of keeping it supplied with the means of heat, at least—and she carried it back into the bigger room, where it quickly began to remove the chill from the atmosphere. Then she returned to the store to conduct an exhaustive search for anything else that might be of comfort to her just then, and found a brown earthenware teapot full of stale tea-leaves, a tin of tea and some sugar, but no milk or anything else apart from a tin kettle filled with water.

She found that the business of emptying the tea-pot, heating the water and making the tea occupied her shaking hands for some little while, and for the time being she thought of nothing but her urgent desire for something hot and reviving inside her. And the tea, drunk out of a cracked cup which she had also discovered, did banish the chill from her weary limbs, and acted like a renewed lease of life, especially while she was thankfully sipping it, although afterwards she felt so pleasantly drowsy that she longed to curl up on the hard, bare floor and go to sleep.

She must have fallen into a doze as she sat on the bench, for when at last she roused herself and looked at her watch it was close upon mid-day. She looked through the window and saw that the mist was still pressing against the front of the cottage, and that if anything it was a trifle thicker than it had been before.

She nodded again, while the warmth of the oil stove filled the room, and all sorts of improbable dreams caught her up like winged things and carried her away from the cottage. There was one in which Iain carried her off, and in which he was so ready to forgive her for running away that it was obvious she had not upset him very greatly by attempting to vanish out of his life. And there was another in which Fiona Barrington lectured her severely for being so stupid as to lose her way, and then ordered her out into the mist again.

She awoke with a little start, realizing that she had been just about to tumble off the bench on to the floor, and then saw by her watch that it was four o'clock in the afternoon. Four o'clock, and the mist had thinned considerably outside, but it was already growing dark, and she didn't think she could risk losing her way a second time by venturing forth in that uncertain light, and with the mist liable to clamp down again at any moment.

It would be better to remain where she was until morning at least.

She heated up the remains of the water and made herself some more tea, then, resigning herself to having nothing whatever to eat, and feeling hungry at last after so many hours of eating nothing at all, she combed her hair in front of her handbag mirror, decided that her sleep had revived her a good deal, and sat waiting for the night to deepen around her and render the little living-room of the cottage dark except for the light from the oil stove.

Once or twice the thought intruded that since no one knew where she was she *could* have caused a certain amount of consternation at Auchenwiel as a result of her (as she now viewed it) extremely undignified action. She had been so kindly treated that her act of running away was rather like an ungrateful visitor departing without thanks. It horrified her to think that she might be thought ungrateful. She did not dare to dwell consciously upon the thought of Iain at all, for whatever his recations to her departure he was the man she would never stop loving with all her heart and soul, and without him the future was bare and bereft as a wintry prospect.

And despite her determination not to think of him she was just beginning to ask herself whether — whether perhaps—he might, on the discovery of her note, have been just a little upset—concerned was the more likely word—when a noise outside the closed front door brought her upright on the bench, and as the door opened all her pulses started to clamor wildly.

Iain stood looking at her with so much sternness on his face that it was almost unrecognizable, and if he was relieved because he had run her to earth it certainly was not given away by his expression.

"So here you are!" he said.

Just four words, but they rang like a kind of knell on her ears, and as he moved towards her she rose in a kind of panic to confront him.

CHAPTER NINETEEN

"I'D HAVE FOUND you before, but the fog was too thick," Iain said, and even his voice was the voice of a stranger—polite, but not particularly concerned. "We searched this morning, after we found you were not with Ellen McBain, and the search has gone on all day, hampered by this confounded mist. How long have you been here?" She thought that he looked pale, and his eyes were hard and frosty as he studied her. "You seem to have made yourself quite comfortable," glancing at the stove.

"I—y-yes——" She didn't know what to answer, or how to answer, and her heart was laboring so heavily that she thought he must hear it in the quiet of the little room. With a purely mechanical gesture she put both her hands up over it, as if an attempt to clutch at it, and at the same time she, too, lost so much color that her eyes looked enormous in the dim lights. "There was no wood, but I found this stove. I've been here for hours——"

"Then you didn't spend much time out there on the moor?"

"No." There was little point in telling him how long she had wandered before she stumbled by accident across the cottage—their cottage, as she had once thought of it—and, in any case, he didn't look as if such a piece of information would particularly interest him. He looked like a judge who had found a prisoner guilty, and was not prepared to hear anything that would soften the punishment he had decided upon. This was at once so clear to Karen that her legs began to feel weakly incapable of supporting her body, and she sank down again on the bench from which she had only just risen.

"Have you had anything to eat?" he asked curtly. "I suppose you haven't."

"I—I made some tea," she admitted. "There was some in a tin——"

But before she could say anything more he had turned and left her, and she heard his footsteps moving away down the path, and the garden gate clicking. Then she distinctly caught the sound of a car door opening and closing, and when he came back to her he was carrying a thermos flask and a heavy plaid rug which he held out to her.

"You'd better wrap that round you," he said. "It strikes warm in her after the air outside, but you've been sitting here for hours and you're probably chilled. As soon as you've had some of this hot coffee I'll get you into the car and take you back to Auchenwiel—for tonight, at least. Tomorrow you'll probably like to join your Nannie McBain."

As he poured the coffee the full implication of his words struck her like a douche of cold water. Although it was true that she herself had taken the initiative and run away in a childish manner—a pitiably childish and undignified manner, as she realized now!— and left him with only the most uninformative of notes to explain why she had done so, somehow in her innermost being there had been an unacknowledged confidence that he never would actually let her go! How, otherwise, had she been able to run away from him?—when the mere sight of him, with his dear, dark head and his strong, dark face, the quiet lines of the mouth she loved so much, the thick eyelashes that hid the grey eyes as he concentrated on the task of pouring her coffee, was enough to set her trembling like an aspen with the realization of what she might have lost? *Might* have lost—?

There was no doubt about it now—she *had* lost him! By her own act—by her complete lack of consideration, not only for him but for his aunt, who had befriended her; she had done something so strongly opposed to his own nature and the code he set himself that even the thought of her as someone with whom he might have to spend the rest of his life was a distasteful idea which he recoiled from.

She held out a shaking hand for the coffee, and managed to take a few gulps without spilling it. He started to pace up and down the little room behind the bench.

"That note you left," he remarked, almost casually. "Fiona was able to shed a certain amount of light on it, because apparently she had a talk with you last night. She had no idea at the time that you were capable of anything so dramatic as stealing out of the house before any of us were up, but at least she was honest enough to come to me and tell me what had happened."

"She — *told* you?" Karen managed to articulate, as if in unbelief. "She told you that I—that she——?"

"Oh," he answered, looking at her with a faint uplifting of his eyebrows, "we've known each other for so long that we've never really had very many secrets from one another. Fiona is a bit impetuous, that's all—but she knows now that I decided long ago that so far as she and I were concerned marriage would never again be in the picture. No one with any sense touches a live electric wire twice, and in the course of time one learns that the live electric wire was there for a purpose. In my case it almost certainly saved me from a disastrous marriage."

"Then—then you——" Karen shifted the beaker of coffee from one hand to the other, and did not dare to lift her eyes above the level of the stove—"You hadn't planned to ask her to marry you again before you met me?"

"I certainly hadn't! I had no thought of marrying anyone when I met you."

There was a silence, while she wondered whether any young woman in the whole world, of her age and with so much offered to her, had behaved with such crass stupidity! More than that, she had so disbelieved in the love that was offered to her that she had poured scorn on it by accepting without question the word of another woman that it was not really hers, and never would be hers. And by so doing the affront she had offered to Iain was surely unforgivable?

He suddenly ceased his restless pacing, and stood looking down at her.

"Now that we've cleared that little matter up," he said, "and if you've finished your coffee, I think we ought to go. It's clear now, but the mist might sweep down again at any moment."

"Yes—very well." She stood up at once, and still without looking at him she handed over the empty flask. She felt so deathly miserable in that moment that she did not notice his eyes alight upon the ring she was wearing on the third finger of her left hand. It was her engagement ring, and even in the dim light from the stove the opal revealed a dozen lovely colors, and the diamonds were sparkling like starshine.

"I see," he observed, in a very cool, strange voice, "that you're still wearing my ring! Isn't the usual procedure to wrap it up in the note that you leave behind and hope tacitly that you'll receive it back in due course through the post as a little momento of what might have been? But I suppose you left so hurriedly that you never thought of that?"

For the first time Karen was stung to the point of feeling a wounded indignation rising up in her, and for the first time she lifted her eyes to his face, and the blue and the grey ones met and continued to meet for perhaps a full half second. Then a flood of painful color rushed into her cheeks. Her lip quivered, and to stop it quivering she caught it up fiercely between her teeth, so that a drop of blood spurted.

"I—I did forget——" she stammered, and made a quick wrench at her finger and removed the ring. She held it out to him. "I'm so sorry," she told him, barely above a whisper.

Coolly he accepted the ring and dropped it into his pocket.

"Thank you," he said.

Karen turned away and took a few blind steps towards the door. She reached out just as blindly for the handle, and her fingers were grasping it and she was striving ineffectually to turn it when she heard him come quietly up behind her. The subtle change in his tone would have escaped her, but his hand grasping her arm was real enough.

"Wait a moment," he commanded her. "I want to ask you something before we go out to the car. I want to ask you how you would have felt if I had behaved as you behaved to me this morning? Even allowing for the fact that Fiona probably upset you last night—and I think that was what she intended to do!—had you so little belief in me that you preferred to believe her before me? Had you so little thought for what I might feel that you considered my reactions to your departure, without any clue as to where I might find you, were not really worth bothering your head about?"

Karen turned to him then and looked up at him. Her face was anguished, and his words had filled her with so much acute distress that it was well-nigh impossible for her to say anything at all in her own defence. And she hadn't really got any defence, because she hadn't considered him, and only now was she realizing just what she might have done to him.

"I know that—that my running away was inexcusable," she managed at last. "But it wasn't because I wanted to hurt you! I would never willingly do that. Only I've always felt that, by comparison with Mrs. Barrington, I had so little to offer you. And she pointed out that I had placed you in an impossible position, and that you were too kind ever to let me think that I had. She told me that if I married you I would be ruining three lives, and I couldn't bear to ruin yours."

"So you decided it had better be your own?"

Her eyes were rather dazed as they gazed back at him—dazed and weary and utterly unhappy.

"It didn't seem to matter so much about me."

She turned away again, her shoulders drooping, and once again she started to fumble with the door handle.

"Karen!" he exclaimed, and because she could not see him she could not tell whether it was exasperation that filled his voice, annoyance, indignation, or a blend of all three—spiced with something that might have been a peculiar brand of humor. "When you're my wife will you promise me you'll stop having such a humble opinion of yourself? And will you also promise me you'll have a little more regard for my feelings, because my opinion of you is almost exactly the same as it was when I first saw you, and the value I place on you is rather high!"

"Oh!" Karen exclaimed, and spun around to stare at him unbelievingly. Her eyes hung upon his dizzily, imploringly, and then with a sudden radiant light in them: "You mean—you don't mean——?"

"I do," he answered, so quietly that she uttered a sound between a gasp and a sob.

Then she was in his arms, and clinging to him. His lips were on hers, and he was kissing her wildly, impetuously, almost despairingly, as if her loss was something he knew only too well could never be repaired, and he had been so terrified that he had lost her that when he found her he could not resist the temptation to punish her just a little.

CHAPTER TWENTY

THE PORTER WAS stowing the light luggage away on the rack, while the heavier luggage, including several pigskin suitcases and a trunk or two, was already disposed in the guard's van. The compartment was first-class, and looking about it Karen realized that this was the first time she had travelled in so much comfort, unless, in the days before she could remember things clearly and before her parents had suffered their disastrous financial crash, they had found it unnecessary to limit themselves to third-class tickets when they journeyed from place to place.

She sat down in a corner seat, while Iain rewarded the porter—who was none other than the man who should have relieved her of her ticket on the night she first arrived in Inverlochie, and who was looking at her with a polite, pleased smile of recognition in his eyes—for his exertions. And then he crossed over and sat beside his very newly-made wife, while the porter slammed the door upon them, and the train started to move slowly out of Inverlochie station.

Once again the steep High Street was bathed in late afternoon sunshine, and once again the narrow church steeple was silhouetted against a background of jagged purple mountain and rose-flushed sky. The woods clothing the lower slopes were greener now, and there were bright flashes of running water finding their way down from the heights, and all the burns around Inverlochie were rippling with movement, too. And the air was much milder—it was no longer freezingly cold.

Iain sat looking closely at his wife as she averted her face from him and watched the tiny platform slide away from them. She was wearing a pearl-grey outfit, and a little jewel-blue velvet cap which clung closely to the back of her head and allowed her soft, fair curls to escape below it and form a kind of nimbus about her face. Her skin looked soft like the petals of a flower, and there was an unmistakable light blush on her cheeks, and her long eyelashes were inclined to droop over her eyes.

Iain said quietly:

"Well, Mrs. Mackenzie! There's no backing out now!"

Karen turned to him at once, and her shyness vanished as if it had never been. She answered him reproachfully:

"As if I would want to back out! As if I *could* want to back out!"

He smiled at her and put his fingers under her chin and lifted it.

"So sure?" he asked.

"I couldn't be more sure!"

A vivid flush of earnestness overspread her face, and her eyes gleamed at him under her lashes with the same jewel-like brilliance as her blue velvet hat. Her mouth looked soft and tremulous — and very, very inviting.

He kissed it, softly, lingeringly.

"I've told you so many times I love you," he said hoarsely. "I shall go on repeating it at intervals throughout our lives, but I hope you'll never again disbelieve me when I say it. You won't, will you, my darling?"

And because the way she looked at him was sufficient answer in itself he caught her into his arms and buried his face against the softness of her hair. He kissed her again, only not so gently this time, and when at last he lifted his head her lips were tingling and scarlet from the almost bruising contact with his. His grey eyes looked dark and brooding like the summits of the mountains surrounding Craigie House.

"I love you, I love you," he said.

"I love you," Karen answered, clinging to him almost fiercely. "I'll never stop loving you!"

"If you ever do, I promise you I'll punish you much more severely than I did yesterday afternoon!"

"Was it only yesterday afternoon?" She put back her head against his shoulder and looked up at him. It was incredible that so much had happened since he had come to her out of the mist and the dusk of only the afternoon before. He had taken her back to Auchenwiel and handed her once more over to the care of his aunt, who had reproached her neither by word nor look, while Fiona was no longer a member of the household, and seemed to have been called away hurriedly for some reason.

Iain had stated quite bluntly that he was no longer prepared to wait even a few days to marry Karen.

"I can't trust you," he said. "I can't trust you either to look after yourself or to behave sensibly, and as I can't trust anybody else to look after you I'm going to marry you straight away. And I'm not going to take you back to Craigie House yet — in spite of what you said to me before I went to London. I want to get away from here for a bit, somewhere where we won't have any reminders of the past nightmarish hours spent looking for you." And because there was something almost haggard in his face when he said this she yielded at once, bitterly reproaching herself because it was she who had caused him so much unnecessary suffering. And as to their return to Craigie House—well, that would be something to which they could look forward when they had wandered for a while in the sun-filled lands he wanted to show to her. It was his wish that she should see them with him, and she had no other conscious thought but that by agreeing with everything he suggested she would be making him as blissfully happy as she was herself.

And if he had suggested honeymooning on a desert island, where there were few amenities, and no comforts, she would have been just as happy.

The minister was contacted and the wedding took place at noon on the morning of the day after her lonely adventure on the moor. And afterwards, while Aunt Horry's maid packed for her hurriedly, and Iain's things were assembled for him hastily at Craigie House, they had a very pleasant lunch at Auchenwiel. The health of the bride and bridegroom was drunk in champagne, and Aunt Horry was a little misty-eyed because Karen, she thought, was such a lovely bride, even if she didn't wear white and carry a bouquet, and she did somehow manage to look almost too young to be embracing all the responsibilities which the acceptance of a wedding ring would inevitably place on her slender shoulders.

After lunch they drove into the village, and Karen said goodbye to Ellen McBain, and received her congratulations at the same time. Ellen whispered to her before they left:

"I told you it would be all right, didn't I?"

And now here they were in the train, and this time tomorrow night she would be in London again with Iain, and the following night in Paris. And after that she didn't quite know where she would be, but it was all almost unbelievable, because wherever she went Iain would be with her. She was his wife!

"Have you fully realized yet that you now possess a husband?" Iain asked her, as the train got into its stride and roared on its way southwards.

Karen's ready color stung her cheeks.

"I—I haven't had much time to do so, have I?" she answered, wishing he would give her the opportunity to hide her face, but his fingers were ruthlessly holding her face up into the open.

He smiled, and there was something more than a slightly quizzical amusement under his thick eyelashes.

"That reminds me," he said. "I'd better go and make sure our sleeper arrangements are all right, and if we're to have any dinner I'd better check up on that, too. But the sleeper is important. I can't have you repeating that extraordinary performance you put up when you travelled north three months ago—sitting up all night in a railway compartment!"

And then because she blushed so vividly he caught her back into his arms and kissed her with almost fierce tenderness.